This month, Harlequin Desire celebrates its 35th anniversary!
Thank you, reader, for being a part of our story!

* * *

"No sex—with anyone. No scandals. Or no 'I do.'"

If no sex was important to her, how could he refuse? "Six weeks," he said hoarsely. "While we're engaged. Once we're married, all bets are off."

"We'll see. You and I don't make sense together, Hendrix, so don't pretend that we do."

She swallowed that sentence with a squeak as he hauled her out of the chair and into his arms for a lesson on exactly how wrong she was.

* * *

One Night Stand Bride is part of the
In Name Only trilogy:

"I do" should solve all their problems,
but love has other plans...

Dear Reader,

I'm thrilled to celebrate the 35th anniversary of Harlequin Desire and even more thrilled that I was able to fulfill my dream of writing for a Harlequin line. I began reading Harlequin romances when I was ten years old and instantly fell in love. I was determined to one day write for one of the lines and I couldn't have been more excited when I was given the chance to write for Harlequin Desire.

Harlequin Desire has published so many wonderful authors over the years, and to say that I'm in good company would be a vast understatement. The stories are full of drama, excitement, passion and romance. I was even more fortunate to also participate in the 30th anniversary celebration in 2012 when the third book of my Pregnancy and Passion miniseries was published as part of the festivities.

The best part of being a Harlequin author is interacting with the readers who love dramatic, sweet, tender and angst-filled stories just as much as I do. And it's because of you, readers, that Harlequin Desire is still going strong after thirty-five years.

So it's with great gratitude that I express my appreciation for each one of you. Thank you for loving Harlequin Desire as much as I do. I have no doubt that the best is yet to come. Please join me in celebrating thirty-five years of excellence, and here's to another thirty-five years of beautiful, romantic and exciting stories.

Much love,

Maya Banks

Xoxo

KAT CANTRELL

ONE NIGHT STAND BRIDE

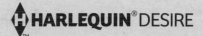

Recycling programs
for this product may
not exist in your area.

ISBN-13: 978-0-373-83877-6

One Night Stand Bride

Printed in U.S.A.

www.Harlequin.com

USA TODAY bestselling author **Kat Cantrell** read her first Harlequin novel in third grade and has been scribbling in notebooks since she learned to spell. She's a Harlequin So You Think You Can Write winner and a Romance Writers of America Golden Heart® Award finalist. Kat, her husband and their two boys live in north Texas.

Books by Kat Cantrell

Harlequin Desire

Marriage with Benefits
The Things She Says
The Baby Deal
Pregnant by Morning
The Princess and the Player
Triplets Under the Tree
The SEAL's Secret Heirs
An Heir for the Billionaire
The Marriage Contract

Love and Lipstick

The CEO's Little Surprise
A Pregnancy Scandal
The Pregnancy Project
From Enemies to Expecting

In Name Only

Best Friend Bride
One Night Stand Bride

Visit her Author Profile page at Harlequin.com, or katcantrell.com, for more titles.

Dear Reader,

Happy anniversary, Harlequin Desire! We're celebrating thirty-five years of amazing books all month long, so don't miss out on the great things in store for our loyal readers. It's always been my dream to be an author for Harlequin, and you've helped make that dream a reality. Thank you, readers!

I hope you're enjoying the In Name Only series as much as I am. I love marriage-of-convenience stories, especially when the stakes are high, and what bigger stakes can there be than political ambitions?

Our second book stars Hendrix Harris, playboy extraordinaire, who secretly longs to be part of something legitimate and real. He gets his chance when one illicit night in Vegas with Rosalind Carpenter threatens to blow his mom's gubernatorial campaign sky-high. Marrying Roz to make the scandal go away is a no-brainer—as long as she doesn't find out he's doing it for his own reasons! Roz has her reasons for agreeing to this marriage, too, and only some of them have to do with clowns. Yes, clowns! No spoilers. Go read about one of my favorite heroines for yourself, and see how she dismantles Hendrix's aversion to love that sprang from the tragedy he and his two friends endured their senior year in college.

Stay tuned as the next book in the series, starring Warren, who's the most resistant to falling in love of the three friends, comes to you soon. Find me online at katcantrell.com and let me know which of my stories you like the best so I can write more of those!

Kat Cantrell

One

The Las Vegas tourism department needed to change their slogan because what happened in Vegas did *not* stay there. In fact, what had happened in Vegas followed Hendrix Harris home to North Carolina and landed above the fold on every media outlet known to man.

He wanted his money refunded, a spell to wipe the memories of an entire city and an aspirin.

Though even he had to admit the photographer had perfectly captured the faces of Hendrix and Rosalind Carpenter. The picture was erotic without being pornographic—a trick and a half since it was abundantly clear they were both buck naked, yet somehow, all the naughty bits were strategically covered. A miracle that had allowed the picture to be print-worthy. It was a one-in-a-million shot. You could even see the steam rising from the hot tub.

And thanks to that photographer being in the right place at the wrong time, Hendrix's luck had run out.

He'd fully expected his mother to have a heart attack when she saw her son naked with the daughter of the wealthiest man in North Carolina. Especially since Hendrix's mother had warned him to keep his clothes on once she launched her gubernatorial campaign.

Joke was on Hendrix. No heart attacks. Instead, his mother was thrilled. *Thrilled* that he'd gotten chummy with Paul Carpenter's daughter. So thrilled that somehow she'd gotten Hendrix to agree that marrying Rosalind would fix everything.

Really, this whole scandal was his fault, and it was on him to make amends, or so he'd been told. The Carpenter family had old money and lots of influence, which provided a nice balance to the Harris new money.

Grumbling in his head because he loved and respected his mother too much to do it out loud, Hendrix threw himself into the task of figuring out how to contact Roz. Their naked Vegas romp had been most definitely of the one-night stand variety. Now he would have to convince her that she loved his mother's plan.

Hendrix didn't hate the idea of marriage, per se, not when it solved more than one problem. So it was now his goal to make sure a big fat yes was Roz's response to the question *Will you marry me?*

The only problem being that he hadn't actually spoken to her since that night and they'd expressly agreed they wouldn't see each other again. Minor detail. When he put his mind to something, rare was the obstacle that didn't get the hell out of his way.

Luck crept back onto his side. Roz hadn't blocked all the web crawlers that posted her address to one of those seamy "find anyone for a price" sites. Hendrix had no qualms about throwing money at this problem.

Hendrix drove himself to the building Rosalind Carpenter lived in on Fayetteville Street instead of taking a car. Arriving with fanfare before he'd gotten this done didn't fit his idea of a good plan. After she said yes, of course there'd be lots of sanctioned pictures of the happy couple. And they'd be dressed.

His mother hadn't properly appreciated just how hard her son had worked to get his abs to look so centerfold-worthy. It was a shame that such a great shot of what had been a truly spectacular night with the hottest woman he'd ever met had done so much damage to Ms. Harris's family values campaign.

He charmed his way past the security desk because everyone liked him instantly, a fact of life he traded on frequently. Then he waited patiently until someone with the right access to Roz's floor who was also willing to listen to his tale of woe got on the elevator. Within fifteen minutes, he knocked on Ms. Carpenter's door.

To her credit, when she answered, she didn't even blink.

He did.

Holy hell. How could he have forgotten what she did to him?

Her sensuality leaped from her like a tidal wave, crashing over him until he scarcely knew which way was up, but he didn't care because surfacing was the last thing on his mind. He gasped for air in the wake of so much sensation as she tucked a lock of dark hair behind her ear. She pursed those lush lips and surveyed him with cool amusement.

"You don't follow instructions well," she fairly purred, leaning on the door, kicking one foot to the side and drawing attention to the sexy slice of leg peeking out from her long flowy skirt.

"Your memory is faulty," he returned easily, a smile sliding across his face in spite of the reason for his visit. "I recall being an instant slave to your instructions. 'Faster, harder, take me from behind.' I can't think of a single thing you told me to do that I didn't follow to the letter."

One dark brow rose. "Other than the one where I said Vegas was a onetime thing?" she reminded him with a wry twist of her lips. "That there were reasons we shouldn't hook up at home and you agreed."

Hendrix waved that off with a grin. "Well, if you're going to get into specifics. Sure. That was the only one, though."

"Then I guess the only thing left to do is ask to what do I owe the pleasure?" That's when she blinked. "Perhaps I should rephrase the question since I have the distinct impression this is not a social call."

No point in dragging it out when they were both to blame for the scandal and they both had a vested interest in fixing the problem. But he did take a moment to appreciate how savvy she was. Contrary to what the majority of women in the Raleigh-Durham-Cary area would argue, Hendrix did notice when a woman had assets outside of the obvious ones.

Roz's brain turned him on. She saw things—layers—that normal people took at face value. It was captivating. He still wasn't sure why it had taken a trip to Vegas for them to hook up when they'd known each other peripherally for years.

"You saw the picture," he said.

"Along with half of the eastern seaboard. But it's been circulating for a week." She slid a once-over down his body, lingering along the way like she'd found something worth noting. "Not sure why that would suddenly cause you to seek me out now."

The region under her hot gaze woke up in a hurry, galvanized into action by the quick, sharp memories of this woman under his mouth as he'd kissed, licked and tasted his way over every inch of her luscious body.

"We're definitely going to have to do something about your defective memory," he growled as he returned her heat with a pointed glance of his own. "If you can look at that photograph and not want to immediately repeat the experience."

She crossed her arms over her filmy top that did little to curb his appetite. "Nothing wrong with my memory and I have no problem admitting that your reputation is well-founded. What's not going to happen is a repeat. Vegas was my last hurrah. I told you that."

Yeah, she had. Repeatedly. While they'd been naked in her bed. And maybe once in the shower. It had been an all-night romp that had nearly caused him to miss his friend Jonas's wedding the next morning. But Hendrix had left behind his delectable companion and made it to the chapel on time, assuming he'd never see her again, as instructed.

His mother, Helene Harris, presumptive future Governor of North Carolina, had reset his thinking. It had taken a week to work through the ramifications and about that long to get him on board with the idea of a wedding as the antidote. But he was all in at this point. And he needed Roz to be all in, too.

"Here's the thing. The picture never should have happened. But it did. So we need to mitigate the damage. My mother's people think that's best accomplished by the two of us getting married. Just until the election. Then her people have agreed that we can get a quiet divorce."

Roz laughed and the silky sound tightened all the places that she'd affected so easily by sheer virtue of standing there looking lush and gorgeous.

"Your mom's people, Hendrix? That's so precious."

"Like your dad doesn't have people?" Carpenter Furniture ranked as one of the top-grossing businesses in the world. Her father had been the CEO since its inception thirty years ago. He had people.

The mirth left her face in a snap. "My dad's people aren't spewing nonsense like a *marriage* to fix a nonexistent problem. This conversation is boring me and I have things to do, so if you'll excuse me."

"Not so fast." Hendrix stuck a foot in the door before Roz could slam it in his face. Time to change tactics. "Let me buy you a drink so we can discuss this like rational adults."

"Yeah. You and alcohol creates a rational atmosphere."

Sarcasm dripped from her tone and it was so cute, he couldn't help but grin.

"Aww. That was very nearly an admission of how crazy I can make you."

"And I'm done with this." She nearly took off his foot with the force of the door closing but he didn't yank it free, despite the pinch in his arch.

"Wait, Roz." He dropped his tone into the *you can't resist me even if you try* realm. "Please give me five minutes. Then you can sever my toes all you want."

"Is the word marriage going to come out of your mouth again?"

He hesitated. Without that, there was no reason for him to be here. But he needed her more than she needed him. The trick was to make sure she never realized that.

"Is it really so much of a stretch to contemplate a merger between our families that could benefit us all? Especially in light of the photograph."

Her face didn't relax, but he could tell he had her attention. Pushing on their mutual attraction wasn't the ticket, then. Noted. So he went with logic.

"Can you honestly say you've had no fallout from our…liaison?" he asked. "Because I have or I wouldn't be standing on your doorstep. I know we agreed no contact. I know the reasons why. Things changed."

But not the reasons why. The reasons for no contact were for pure self-preservation.

He and Roz were like kindling dropped into a forest fire together. They'd gone up in flames and frankly, he'd done more dirty things in one night with Rosalind Carpenter than with the last ten women he'd dated. But by the time the sun rose, they were done. He had a strict one-time-only rule that he never broke and not just because of the pact he'd made his senior year at Duke. He'd vowed to never fall in love—because he'd been rejected enough in life and the best way to avoid all that noise was to avoid intimacy.

Sex he liked. Sex worked for him. But intimacy was off the table. He guaranteed it with no repeats.

Only at his mother's insistence would he consider making Roz his onetime exception.

"So this marriage idea. That's supposed to fix the fallout? From where I'm sitting, you're the reason for the scandal. Where's the plus for me?"

Like she hadn't been the one to come on to him on the dance floor of the Calypso Room, with her smoky eyes undressing him, the conclusion of their evening foregone the second their bodies touched.

At least she hadn't denied that the photograph had caused her some difficulty. If she had, he'd remind her that somewhere around 2:00 a.m. that night, she'd confessed that she was looking to change her reputation as the scandalous Carpenter daughter. The photograph couldn't have helped. A respectable marriage would.

That fact was still part of his strategy. "Helene's your plus. You'll be the daughter-in-law of the next governor of North Carolina. I'm confused why you're struggling with this."

"You would be." She jerked her head toward him. "I'm morbidly curious. What's in this for you?"

Legitimacy. Something hard to come by in his world. His family's chain of tobacco shops wasn't a respected industry and he was the bastard son of a man who had never claimed him.

But what he said was, "Sex."

She rolled her eyes. "You're such a liar. The last thing you need to bargain for is a woman willing to get naked with you."

"That sounded like a compliment." He waggled his brows to hide how his insides suddenly felt wobbly and precarious. How had she seen through that flippant answer?

That was what he got with a smart woman, apparently.

"It wasn't. Seduction is less of an art when you're already starting out with the deck stacked."

He had to laugh, though he wasn't quite sure if he was supposed to say thank you for the backhanded nod to his skill set. "I'm not leaving here without an answer. Marry me and the scandal goes away."

She shook her head, a sly smile spreading over her face. "Over my dead body."

And with that, she pushed his foot from the gap and shut the door with a quiet click.

Dumbfounded, Hendrix stared at the fine-grain

wood. Rosalind Carpenter had just rejected his proposal. For deliberately not putting anything emotional on the line, the rejection sure stung.

Roz leaned on the shut door and closed her eyes.
Marriage. To Hendrix Harris. If she hadn't understood perfectly why he'd come up with such a ridiculous idea, she'd call the cops to come cart away the crazy man on her doorstep.

But he wasn't crazy. Just desperate to fix a problem.

She was, too.

The big difference was that her father wasn't working with his "people" to help her. Instead, he was sitting up in his ivory tower continuing to be disappointed in her. Well, sometimes she screwed up. Vegas had been one of those times. Fixing it lay solely at her feet and she planned to. Just not by marrying the person who had caused the scandal in the first place.

Like marriage was the solution to anything, especially marriage to Hendrix Harris, who indeed had a reputation when it came to his exploits with the opposite sex. Hell, half of her interest back on that wild night had been insatiable curiosity about whether he could be as much trouble as everyone said.

She should have run the moment she recognized

him. But no. She'd bought him a drink. She was nothing if not skilled at getting into trouble.

And what trouble she'd found.

He was of the hot, wicked and oh-so-sinful variety—the kind she had a weakness for, the kind she couldn't resist. The real question was how she'd shut the door in his face a moment ago instead of inviting him in for a repeat.

That would be a bad idea. Vegas had marked the end of an era for her.

She'd jetted off with her friend Lora to let loose in a place famed for allowing such behavior without ramifications. One last hurrah, as Roz had informed him. Make it memorable, she'd insisted. *Help me go out with a bang*, had been her exact words. Upon her return to the real world, she'd planned to make her father proud for once.

Instead, she'd found exactly the trouble she'd been looking for and then some.

It was a problem she needed to fix. She'd needed to fix it before she'd ever let Hendrix put his beautiful, talented mouth on her. And now memories of his special brand of trouble put a slow burn in her core that she couldn't shake. Even now, five minutes after telling him to shove off. Still burning. She cursed her weakness for gorgeous bad boys and went to change clothes so she could dig into her "make Dad proud" plan on her terms.

Marriage. Rosalind Carpenter. These two things

did not go together under any circumstances, especially not as a way to make her father proud of her.

After watching her father cope with Roz's mother's extended bout with cancer, no thank you. That kind of pain didn't appeal to her. Till death do you part wasn't a joke, nor did she take a vow like that lightly. Best way to avoid testing it was to never make a vow like that in the first place.

Roz shed the flirty, fun outfit she'd worn to brunch with Lora and donned a severe black pencil skirt coupled with a pale blue long-sleeved blouse that screamed "serious banker." She twisted her long hair into a chignon, fought with the few escaped strands and finally left them because Hendrix had already put her behind for the day. Her afternoon was booked solid with the endless tasks associated with the new charity she'd founded.

She arrived at the small storefront her father's admin had helped her rent, evaluating the layout for the fourteenth time. There was no sign yet. That was one of the many details she needed to work through this week as she got Clown-Around off the ground. It was an endeavor of the heart. And maybe a form of therapy.

Clowns still scared her, not that she'd admit to having formed a phobia during the long hours she'd sat at her mother's hospital bedside, and honestly, she didn't have to explain herself to anyone, so she didn't. The curious only needed to know that

Rosalind Carpenter had started a charity that trained clowns to work in children's hospitals. Period.

The desk she'd had delivered dwarfed her, but she'd taken a page from her father's book and procured the largest piece she could find in the Carpenter warehouse near the airport. He'd always said to buy furniture for the circumstances you want, not the ones you have. Buy quality so it will last until you make your dreams a reality. It was a philosophy that had served Carpenter Furniture well and she liked the sentiment. So she'd bought a desk that made her feel like the head of a successful charity.

She attacked the mountain of paperwork with gusto, cheerfully filling out forms and ordering supplies. There was an enormous amount of overhead that went along with running a charity and when you had zero income to use in hiring help, there was only one person to do the work—the founder.

Before she'd barely dug into the task, the lady from the first hospital Roz had called her back.

"Ms. Smith, so happy to speak with you," Roz began smoothly. "I'd like to see what your requirements are for getting Clown-Around on the approved list of organizations available to work with the children at your hospital."

"I could have saved you some time, Ms. Carpenter," the liaison replied and her tone could only be described as frosty. "We already have an approved group we work with. No need for any additional ones."

That threw Roz for a loop. "Oh. Well, we'd be happy to go on the backup list. You know, in case the other group cancels unexpectedly."

"That's okay," she cut in quickly. "That almost never happens and it's not like we have scheduled times. The clowns come in on a pretty casual basis."

This was not a good conversation. Unease prickled at the back of Roz's neck and she did not like the feeling. "I'm having a hard time believing that you can't use extra cheer in the children's ward. We're talking about sick kids who don't want to be in the hospital. Surely if your current clowns come and go at will, you can add some of mine to the rotation. A clown is a clown, right?"

The long pause boded badly. Roz braced for the next part.

"To be frank, Ms. Carpenter, the hospital board would not appreciate any association with a charity you helm," Ms. Smith stated bluntly. "We are required to disclose any contact a patient has with outside parties, particularly when the patients are minors. The clowns must have accreditation and thorough vetting to ensure we're not exposing patients to…unseemly influences."

Roz went hot and then cold as the woman's meaning flashed through her. The reputation of the charity's founder preceded her apparently. "I take it I qualify as an unseemly influence. Then may I be as frank and ask why you bothered to call me back?"

"Strictly in deference to your father. One of his vice presidents is on the board, if you're not aware," she replied tightly. "If we've reached an understanding…"

"We have. Thank you for your candor." Roz stabbed the end call button and let her cell phone drop to the desk of a successful charity head. Too bad that wasn't who was sitting at it.

Wow. Her hands were shaking.

And because her day hadn't been crappy enough, the door she'd forgotten to lock behind her opened to the street and Hendrix Harris walked into her nightmare.

"What are you doing here?" she snapped, too off-kilter to find some manners when she'd already told him to step off once today. "This is private property. How did you find me?"

Not one perfect brown hair out of place, the man waltzed right in and glanced around her bare-bones operation with unabashed curiosity. "I followed you, naturally. But I didn't want to interrupt your phone call, so I waited."

"Bless your heart," she shot back and snatched up her phone to call the cops. "You have two seconds to vacate or I'm going to lodge a trespassing complaint."

Instead of hightailing it out the door—which was what he should have done—Hendrix didn't hesitate to round the desk, crowd into her space without even a cursory nod to boundaries and pluck the phone from her hand. "Now, why would you do a thing like that? We're all friends here."

Something that felt perilously close to tears pricked beneath her lashes. "We're not friends."

Tears. In front of Hendrix. It was inexcusable.

"We could be friends," he announced quietly, without an ounce of flirt. Somehow that was exactly the right tone to burn off the moisture. "Friends who help each other. You didn't give me much of a chance to tell you how earlier."

Help. That was something she needed. Not that *he* needed to know that, or how grateful she was that he'd found a way to put her back on even footing. She didn't for an instant believe he'd missed her brief flash of vulnerability and his deft handling of it made all the difference.

The attitude of the hospital lady still chilled her. But she wasn't in danger of falling apart any longer, thank God.

"Because I have a zone of crazy around me." She nodded to the floor, near his feet. "There's the perimeter and you're four feet over the line."

Problem being that she liked him where he was—one lean hip cocked against her desk and all his good stuff at eye level. Naked, the man rivaled mythical gods in the perfection department. She could stare at his bare body for hours and never get tired of finding new ways to appreciate his deliciousness.

And dang it, he must have clued in on the direction of her thoughts. He didn't move. But the temperature of the room rose a few sweat-inducing degrees. Or maybe that was just her body catching fire as he treated her to the full force of his lethal appeal.

His hot perusal did not help matters when it came to the temperature. What was it about his pale hazel eyes that dug into her so deeply? All he had to do was look at her and sharp little tugs danced through her core.

It pissed her off. Why couldn't he be ugly, with a hunchback and gnarled feet?

Which was a stupid thing to wish for because if that was the case, she wouldn't be in this position. She'd never have hooked up with him in Vegas because yes, she was that shallow and a naked romp with a man built like Hendrix had righted her world—for a night.

Now she'd pay the price for that moment of hedonism. The final cost had yet to be determined, though.

Hendrix set her phone down on the desk, correctly guessing he had her attention and the threat of expulsion had waned. For now. She could easily send him packing if the need struck. Or she could roll the chair back a few inches and move the man into a better position to negotiate something of the more carnal variety. This was a solid desk. Would be a shame not to fully test its strength.

No. She shook her head. This was the danger of putting herself in the same room with him. She forgot common sense and propriety.

"Since I'm already in the zone of crazy," he commented in his North Carolina–textured twang, "you should definitely hear me out. For real this time. I don't know what you think I'm proposing, but odds are good you didn't get that it starts and ends with a partnership."

That had *not* come across. Whatever he had in mind, she'd envisioned a lot of sex taking center stage. And that she'd have to do without because she'd turned over a new leaf.

A partnership, on the other hand, had interesting possibilities.

As coolly as she could under the circumstances, she crossed her arms. Mostly as a way to keep her hands to herself. "Talk fast. You've got my attention for about another five minutes."

Two

Hendrix had been right to follow Rosalind. This bare storefront had a story behind it and he had every intention of learning her secrets. Whatever leverage he could dig up might come in handy, especially since he'd botched the first round of this negotiation.

And the hard cross of Roz's arms told him it was indeed a negotiation, one he shouldn't expect to win easily. That had been his mistake on the first go-round. He'd thought their chemistry would be good trading currency, but she'd divested him of that notion quickly. So round two would need a completely different approach.

"What is this place?" he asked and his genuine curiosity leaked through. He had a vision in his head of Rosalind Carpenter as a party girl, one who posed for men's magazines and danced like a fantasy come to life. Instead of tracking her down during an afternoon shopping spree, he'd stumbled over her *working*.

It didn't fit his perception of her and he'd like to get the right one before charging ahead.

"I started a charity," she informed him with a slight catch in her voice that struck him strangely.

She expected him to laugh. Or say something flippant. So he didn't. "That's fantastic. And hard. Good for you."

That bobbled her composure and he wouldn't apologize for enjoying it. This marriage plan should have been a lot easier to sell and he couldn't put his finger on why he'd faltered so badly thus far. She'd been easy in Vegas—likable, open, adventurous. All things he'd assumed he'd work with today, but none of those qualities seemed to be a part of her at-home personality. Plus, he wasn't trying to get her into bed. Well, technically, he *was*. But semi-permanently, and he didn't have a lot of experience at persuading a woman to still be there in the morning.

No problem. Winging it was how he did his best work. He hadn't pushed Harris Family Tobacco Lounge so close to the half-billion mark in revenue without taking a few risks.

"What does your charity do?" he asked, envisioning an evening dress resale shop or Save the Kittens. Might as well know what kind of fundraiser he'd have to attend as her husband.

"Clowns," she said so succinctly that he did a double take to be sure he hadn't misheard her. He hadn't. And it wasn't a joke, judging by the hard set of her mouth.

"Like finding new homes for orphan clowns?" he guessed cautiously, only half kidding. Clown charity was a new one for him.

"You're such a moron." She rolled her eyes, but they had a determined glint now that he liked a lot better than the raw vulnerability she'd let slip a few minutes ago. "My charity trains clowns to work with children at hospitals. Sick kids need to be cheered up, you know?"

"That's admirable." And he wasn't even blowing smoke. It sounded like it meant something to her and thus it meant something to him—as leverage. He glanced around, taking in the bare walls, the massive and oddly masculine dark-stained desk and the rolling leather chair under her very fine backside. Not much to her operation yet, which worked heavily in his favor. "How can I help?"

Suspicion tightened her lush mouth, which only made him want to kiss it away. They were going to have to fix this attraction or he'd spend all his time adjusting her attitude in a very physical way.

On second thought, he couldn't figure out a downside to that approach.

"I thought you were trying to talk me into marrying you," she said with a fair amount of sarcasm.

"One and the same, sweetheart." He gave it a second and the instant his meaning registered, her lips curved into a crafty smile.

"I'm starting to see the light."

Oh yes, *now* they were ready to throw down. Juices flowing, he slid a little closer to her and she didn't roll away, just coolly stared up at him without an ounce of give. What was wrong with him that he was suddenly more turned on in that instant than he had been at any point today?

"Talk to me. What can I do in exchange for your name on a marriage certificate?"

Her smile gained a lot of teeth. "Tell me why it's so important to you."

He bit back the curse. Should have seen that one coming. As a testament to her skill in maneuvering him into giving up personal information, he opted to throw her a bone. "I told you. I've had some fallout. My mother is pretty unhappy with me and I don't like her to be unhappy."

"Mama's boy?"

"Absolutely." He grinned. Who didn't see the value in a man who loved and respected his mama? "There's no shame in that. We grew up together.

I'm sure you've heard the story. She was an unwed teenage mother, yadda, yadda?"

"I've heard. So this is all one hundred percent about keeping your mom happy, is it?"

Something clued him in that she wasn't buying it, which called for some serious deflection. The last thing he wanted to have a conversation about was his own reasons for pursuing Roz for the first and only Mrs. Hendrix Harris.

He liked being reminded of his own vulnerabilities even less than he liked being exposed to hers. The less intimate this thing grew, the better. "Yeah. If she wasn't in the middle of an election cycle, we wouldn't be having this conversation. But she is and I messed up. I'm willing to do whatever it takes to get this deal done. Name your price."

"Get your mom to agree to be a clown for me and I'll consider it."

That was what she wanted? His gaze narrowed as they stared at each other. "That's easy. Too easy. You must not want me to figure out that you're really panting to get back into my bed."

Her long silky laugh lodged in his chest and spread south. She could turn that sentiment back on him with no trouble at all.

Which was precisely what she did. "Sounds like a guilty conscience talking to me. Sure you're not the one using this ploy to get me naked without being forced to let on how bad you want it?"

"I'm offended." But he let a smile contradict the statement. "I'll tell you all day long how much I want you if that floats your boat. But this is a business proposition. Strictly for nonsexual benefits."

Any that came along with this marriage could be considered a bonus.

She snorted. "Are you trying to tell me you'd give up other women while we're married? I don't think you're actually capable of that."

Now, that was just insulting. What kind of a philanderer did she take him for? He'd never slept with more than one woman at a time and never calling one again made that a hundred percent easier.

"Make no mistake, Roz. I am perfectly capable of forgoing other women as long as you're the one I'm coming home to at the end of the day."

All at once, a vision of her greeting him at the door wearing sexy lingerie slammed through his mind and his body reacted with near violent approval. Holy hell. He had no problem going off other women cold turkey if Roz was on offer instead, never mind his stupid rules about never banging the same woman twice. This situation was totally different, with its own set of rules. Or at least it would be as soon as he got his head out of her perfect cleavage and back on how to close this deal.

"Let me get this straight. You're such a dog that the only way you can stay out of another woman's bed is if I'm servicing you regularly?" She wrinkled her nose. "Stop me when I get to the part where I'm benefiting from this arrangement."

Strictly to cover the slight hitch in his lungs that her pointed comment had caused, he slid over until he was perched on the desk directly in front of her. Barely a foot of space separated them and an enormous amount of heat and electricity arced through his groin, draining more of his sense than he would have preferred. All he could think about was yanking her into his arms and reminding her how hot he could get her with nothing more than a well-placed stroke of his tongue.

He let all of that sizzle course through his body as he swept her with a heated once-over. "Sweetheart, you'll benefit, or have you forgotten how well I know your body?"

"Can you even go without sex?" she mused with a lilt, as if she already knew the answer. "Because I bet you can't."

What the hell did that have to do with anything?

"I can do whatever I put my mind to," he growled. "But to do something as insane as go without sex, I'd need a fair bit of incentive. Which I have none of."

Her gaze snapped with challenge. "Other than getting my name on a marriage license you mean?"

The recoil jerked through his shoulders before he could catch it, tipping her off that she'd just knocked him for a loop. That was uncool. Both that she'd realized it and that she'd done it. "What are you proposing, that I go celibate for a period of time in some kind of test?"

"Oh, I hadn't thought of it like that." She pursed her lips into a provocative pout that told him she was flat-out lying because she'd intended it to be exactly that. "That's a great deal. You keep it zipped and I'll show up at the appointed time to say 'I do.'"

His throat went dry. "Really? That's what it's going to take?"

"Yep. Well, that and Helene Harris for Governor in a clown suit. Can't forget the children."

Her smug tone raked at something inside him. "That's ridiculous. I mean, my mom would be happy to do the clown thing. It's great publicity for her, too. But no sex? Not even with you? There is literally no reason for you to lay down such a thing except as cruel and unusual punishment."

"Careful, Hendrix," she crooned. "It's starting to sound like you might have a problem keeping it in your pants. I mean, how long are we talking? A couple of months?"

A couple of *months*? He'd been slightly panicked at the thought of a week or two. It wasn't that he was some kind of pervert like she was making it sound. Sex was a necessary avoidance tactic in his arsenal. A shield against the intimacy that happened in the small moments, when you weren't guarded against it. He kept himself out of such situations on purpose.

If he wasn't having sex with Roz, what would they *do* with each other?

"I think the better question is whether *you* can do it," he countered smoothly. "You're the same woman who was all in for every wicked, dirty escapade I could dream up in Vegas. You're buckling yourself into that chastity belt too, honey."

"Yeah, for a reason." Her eyes glittered with conviction. "The whole point of this is to fix the problems the photograph caused. Do you really think you and I can keep ourselves out of Scandalville if we're sleeping together?" His face must have registered his opinion on that because she nodded. "Exactly. It's a failsafe. No sex—with *anyone*. No scandals. Or no 'I do.'"

The firm press of a rock and a hard place nearly stole his breath. If no sex was important to her, how could he refuse?

"Six weeks," he said hoarsely. "We'll be engaged for six weeks. Once we're married, all bets are off."

"We'll see. I might keep the no sex moratorium. You and I don't make sense together, Hendrix, so don't pretend that we do."

She swallowed that sentence with a squeak as he hauled her out of that chair and into his arms for a lesson on exactly how wrong she was. God, she fit the contours of his body like the ocean against the sand, seeping into him with a rush and shush, dragging pieces of him into her as her lips crashed against his.

Her taste exploded under his mouth as he kissed her senseless. But then it was his own senses sliding through the soles of his feet as Roz sucked him dry with her own sensual onslaught. For a woman who'd just told him they didn't work, she jumped into the kiss with enthusiasm that had him groaning.

The hot, slick slide of her tongue against his dissolved his knees. Only the firm press of that heavy desk against his backside kept him upright. The woman was a wicked kisser, not that he'd forgotten. But just as he slid his hand south to fill his palms with her luscious rear, she wrenched away, taking his composure with her.

"Where are you going?" he growled.

"The other side of the room." Her chest rose and fell as if she'd run a marathon as she backed away. Frankly, his own lungs heaved with the effort to fill with air. "What the hell was that for?"

"You wanted that kiss as much as I did."

"So it was strictly to throw it back in my face that I can't resist you?"

Well, now. That was a tasty admission that she looked like she wished to take back. He surveyed her with renewed interest. Her kiss-reddened lips beckoned him but he didn't chase her down. He wanted to understand this new dynamic before he pressed on. "You said we didn't work. I was simply helping you see the error in that statement."

"I said no such thing. I said we don't make sense together. And that's why. Because we *work* far too well."

"I'm struggling to see the problem with that." They'd definitely worked in Vegas, that was for sure. Now that he'd gotten a second taste, he was not satisfied with having it cut short.

"Because I need to stay off the front page," she reminded him with that funny hitch in her voice that shouldn't be more affecting than her heated once-overs. "There are people walking by the window as we speak, Hendrix. You make me forget all of that. No more kissing until the wedding. Consider it an act of good faith."

The point was painfully clear. She wanted him to prove he could do it.

"So we're doing this. Getting married," he clarified.

"As a partnership. When it stops being beneficial, we get a divorce. No ifs, ands or buts." She caught him in her hot gaze that still screamed her desire. "Right? Do we need to spell it out legally?"

"You can trust me," he grumbled. She was the one who'd thrown down the no-sex rule. What did she think he was going to do, force her to stay married so he could keep being celibate for the rest of his life? "As long as I can trust you."

"I'm good."

He thought about shaking on it but the slightly panicked flair to her expression made him think twice. It didn't matter. The deal was done, as painful as it would ultimately end up being.

It was worth it. He had to make it up to his mom for causing her grief, and this was what she'd asked him to do. And if deep inside, he craved the idea of belonging to such an old-guard, old-money family as the Carpenters, no one would be the wiser.

All he had to do was figure out how to be engaged to Roz without trying to seduce her again and without getting too chummy. Should be a walk in the park.

Being engaged was nothing like Roz imagined. Of course she'd spent zero time daydreaming about such a thing happening to her. But her friend Lora had been engaged for about six months, which had been a whirlwind of invitations and dress fittings. Until the day she'd walked in on her fiancé and a naked barista who was foaming the jackass's latte in Lora's bed. Roz and Lora still didn't hit a coffee place within four blocks of the one where the wedding-wrecker worked.

Roz's own engagement had a lot fewer highs and lows in the emotion department and a lot less chaos. For about three days. The morning of the fourth day, Hendrix texted her that he was coming by, and since there'd been no question in that statement, she sighed and put on clothes, wishing in vain for a do-over that included not flying to Vegas in the first place. Or maybe she should wish that she and Lora had gone to any other club besides the Calypso Room that night.

Oh, better yet, she could pretend Hendrix didn't do it for her in a hundred scandalous ways.

That was the real reason this engagement/marriage/partnership shouldn't have happened. But how could she turn down Helene Harris in a clown outfit? No hospital would bar the woman from the door and thus Clown-Around would get a much-needed lift, Roz's reputation notwithstanding. It was instant publicity for the gubernatorial candidate and the fledgling charity in one shot, which was a huge win. And she didn't have to actually ask her father to use his influence, which he probably wouldn't do anyway.

Plus, and she'd die before she'd admit this to Hendrix, there had to be something about being in the sphere of Helene Harris that Roz's father would find satisfactory. He was so disappointed about the photographs. If nothing else, marrying the man in them lent a bit of respectability to the situation, right? Now Roz just had to tell her father about the getting married part. But first she had to admit to herself that she'd actually agreed to this insanity.

Thus far it had been easy to stick her head in the

sand. But when Hendrix buzzed her to gain access to the elevator, she couldn't play ostrich any longer.

"Well, if it isn't my beloved," he drawled when she opened the door.

God, could the man look like a slouch in *something*? He wore the hell out of a suit regardless of the color or cut. But today he'd opted for a pair of worn jeans that hugged his hips and a soft T-shirt that brazenly advertised the drool-worthy build underneath. He might as well be naked for all that ensemble left to the imagination.

"Your beloved doesn't sit around and wait for you to show up on a Saturday," she informed him grumpily. "What if I had plans?"

"You do have plans," he returned, his grin far too easy. "With me. All of your plans are with me for the next six weeks, because weddings do not magically throw themselves together."

She crossed her arms and leaned against the doorjamb in a blatant message—*you're not coming in and I'm not budging, so...* "They do if you hire a wedding planner. Which you should. I have absolutely no opinion about flowers or venues."

That was no lie. But she wanted to spend time with Hendrix even less than she wanted to pick out flowers. She could literally feel her will dissolving as she stood there soaking in the carnal vibe wafting from him like an invisible aphrodisiac.

"Oh, come on. It'll be fun."

The way his hazel eyes lit up as he coaxed her should be illegal. Or maybe her reaction should be. How did he put such a warm little curl in her core with nothing more than a glance? It was ridiculous. "Your idea of fun and mine are worlds apart."

A slow, lethal smile joined his vibrant gaze and it pretty much reduced her to a quivering mess of girl parts inside. All the more reason to stay far away from him until the wedding.

"Seems like we had a pretty similar idea of fun one night not too long ago."

Memories crashed through her mind, her body, her soul. The way he'd made her feel, the wicked press of his mouth against every intimate hollow an unprecedented experience. It was too much for a Saturday morning after she'd signed up to become Mrs. Hendrix Harris.

"I asked you not to kiss me again," she reminded him primly but it probably sounded as desperate to him as it did to her.

She could *not* get sucked into his orbit. As it was, she fantasized about that kiss against her desk at odd times—while in the shower, brushing her teeth, eating breakfast, watching TV, walking, breathing. Sure it was prudent to avoid any more scandals but that was just window dressing. This was a partnership she needed to take seriously, and she had no good defenses against Hendrix Harris.

He was temporary. Like all things. She couldn't

get invested, emotionally or physically, and one would surely lead to the other. The pain of losing someone she cared about was too much and she would never let that happen again—which was the sole reason she liked sex of the one-night stand variety. What she'd do when that wasn't an option, like after she said I do, she had no clue.

"Wow. Who said anything about kissing?" He waggled his brows. "We were talking about the definition of fun. That kiss must have gotten you going something fierce if you're still hung up on it."

She rolled her eyes to hide the guilt that might or might not be shuffling through her expression. "Why are you here?"

"We're engaged. Engaged people hang out, or didn't you get the memo?"

"We're not people. Nor is our engagement typical. No memos required to get us to the…insert whatever venue we're using to get hitched here. Until then, I don't really feel the need to spend time together." She accompanied that pitiful excuse of his with crooked fingers in air quotes.

"Well, I beg to differ," he drawled, the North Carolina in his voice sliding through her veins like fine brandy. "This partnership needs publicity or there's no point to it. We need to be seen together. A lot. When people think of you, they need to think of me. We're like the peanut butter and jelly of the Raleigh social scene."

"That's a nice analogy," she said with a snort so she didn't laugh or smile. That would only encourage him to keep being adorable. "Which one am I?"

"You choose," he suggested magnanimously and that's when she realized she was having fun. How dare he charm her out of her bad mood?

But it was too late, dang it. That was the problem. She genuinely liked Hendrix or she wouldn't have left the Calypso Room with him.

"I suppose you want to come in." She jerked her head toward the interior of her loft that had been two condos until she bought both and hired a crew of hard hats to meld the space into one. They should probably discuss living arrangements at some point because she was *not* giving up this condo under any circumstances.

"I want you to come out," he countered and caught her hand, tugging on it until she cleared the threshold on the wrong side of the door. "We can't be seen together in your condo and besides, there are no people walking past the window. No photographers in the bushes. I could slip a couple of buttons free on this shirt of yours and explore what I uncover with my tongue and no one would know."

He accompanied that suggestion with a slow slide of his fingertip along the ridge of buttons in question, oh so casually, as if the skin under it hadn't just exploded with goose bumps.

"But you won't," she said breathlessly, cursing her body's reaction even as she cursed him for knowing exactly how to get her hot and ready to burst with so little effort. "Because you promised."

"I did." He nodded with a wink. "And I'm a man of my word."

She'd only reminded him of his promise as a shield against her own weaknesses, but he'd taken it as an affirmation. He would keep his promise because it meant something to him. And his sense of honor was doing funny things to her insides that had nothing to do with desire. Hendrix Harris was a bad boy hedonist of the highest order. Nothing but wicked through and through. Or at least that was the box she'd put him in and she did not like the way he'd just climbed out of it.

She shook her head, but it didn't clear her sudden confusion. Definitely they should not go into her condo and shut the door. Not now or any day. But at that moment, she couldn't recall what bad things might happen as a result. She could only think of many, many very good things that could and would occur if she invited him in for a private rendezvous.

"I think we should visit a florist," he commented casually, completely oblivious to the direction of her thoughts, thank God.

"Yes. We should." That was exactly what she needed. A distraction in the form of flowers.

"Grab your handbag." The instruction made her blink for a second until he laughed. "Or is it a purse? I have no clue what to call the thing you women put your lives into."

Gah, she should have her head examined if a simple conversation with a man had her so flipped upside down. Nodding, she ducked back into the condo, snagged her Marc Jacobs bag from the counter in the kitchen and rejoined Hendrix in the hall before he got any bright ideas about testing his will behind closed doors. Hers sucked. The longer she kept that fact from him, the better.

He ushered her to a low-slung Aston Martin that shouldn't have been as sexy as it was. At best, it should have screamed *I'm trying too hard to be cool.* But when Hendrix slid behind the wheel, he owned the beast under the hood and it purred beneath his masterful hands.

She could watch him drive for hours. Which worked out well since she'd apparently just volunteered to spend the day planning flowers for her wedding with her fiancé. Bizarre. But there it was.

Even she had heard of the florist he drove to. Expensive, exclusive and very visible, Maestro of the Bloom lay in the Roundtree shopping district near downtown. Hendrix drove around the block two times, apparently searching for a parking place, and she opened her mouth to remind him of the lot across the street when he braked at the front row to wait for a mother and daughter to get into their car. Of course he wanted the parking place directly in front of the door, where everyone could see them emerge from his noteworthy car.

It was a testament to his strategic mind that she appreciated. As was the gallant way he sped around to her side of the car to open the door, then extended his hand to help her from the bucket seat that was so low it nearly scraped the ground. But he didn't let go of her hand, instead lacing their fingers together in a way that shouldn't have felt so natural. Hands nested to his satisfaction, he led her to the door and ushered her inside.

A low hum of conversation cut off abruptly and something like a dozen pairs of eyes swung toward them with varying degrees of recognition—some of which held distaste. These were the people whose approval they both sought. The society who had deemed their Vegas tryst shocking, inappropriate, scandalous, and here the two of them were daring to tread among more decent company.

Roz's fingers tightened involuntarily and dang it, Hendrix squeezed back in a surprising show of solidarity. That shouldn't have felt as natural as it did either, like the two of them were a unit already. Peanut butter and jelly against the world.

Her knees got a little wobbly. She'd never had anything like that. Never wanted to feel like a duo with a man. Why did it mean so much as they braved the social scene together? Especially given that she'd only just realized that turning over a new leaf meant more than fixing her relationship with her father. It was about shifting the tide of public opinion too, or her charity wouldn't benefit much from Helene's participation. Roz would go back to being shunned in polite society the moment she signed the divorce papers.

Against all odds, he'd transformed Roz into a righteous convert to the idea of marriage with one small step inside the florist. What else would he succeed in convincing her of?

With that sobering thought, Roz glanced at Hendrix and murmured, "Let's do this."

Three

As practice for the bigger, splashier engagement party to come, Hendrix talked Roz into an intimate gathering at his house. Just family and close friends. It would be an opportunity to gauge how this marriage would fly. And it was a chance to spend time together as a couple with low pressure.

The scene at the florist had shaken Roz, with the murmurs and dirty looks she'd collected from the patrons. That was not okay. Academically, he knew this marriage deal was important to his mother and her campaign. In reality, he didn't personally have a lot of societal fallout from that photo. No one's gaze cut away from him on the street, but he was a guy. Roz wasn't. It was a double standard that shouldn't exist but it did.

Who would have ever thought he'd be hot to ease Roz's discomfort in social situations? It had not been on his list of considerations, but it was now. If this party helped, great. If it didn't, he'd find something else. The fragile glint in her eye while they'd worked with the florist to pick out some outrageously priced flowers had hooked something inside and he'd spent a considerable amount of time trying to unpierce his tender flesh, to no avail. So he did what he always did. Rolled with it.

The catering company had done a great job getting his house in order to host a shindig of this magnitude. While the party had been floated as casual, Hendrix had never entertained before. Unless you counted a handful of buddies sprawled around his dining room table with beer and poker chips.

Roz arrived in the car he'd sent for her and he ignored the little voice inside taunting him for hovering at the front window to watch for her. But it was a sight to see. Roz spilled from the back of the car, sky-high stilettos first, then miles of legs and finally the woman herself in a figure-hugging black cocktail dress designed to drive a man insane.

She'd even swept up her wavy dark hair into a chignon that let a few strands drip down around her face. It was the sexiest hairstyle he'd ever seen on a woman, bar none.

He opened the door before she could knock and his tongue might have gone numb because he couldn't even speak as she coolly surveyed him from under thick black eyelashes.

"Thanks for the car. Hard to drive in heels," she commented, apparently not afflicted by the stupid that was going around.

He shouldn't be, either. He cleared his throat. "You look delicious."

Amazing might have been a better term. It would make it seem more like he'd seen a beautiful woman before and it was no big thing. But she was *his* beautiful woman. For as long as they both deemed it beneficial.

That seemed like a pretty cold agreement all at once for two people who'd burned so very hot not so long ago.

She smiled with a long slow lift of her pink-stained lips. "I'll take that as a compliment, as weird as it is."

"Really? It's weird to tell my beautiful fiancée that she looks good enough to eat?" he questioned with a heated once-over that she didn't miss.

"You can't say stuff like that," she murmured and glanced away from the sizzling electricity that had just arced between them right there on his doorstep.

"The hell I can't. You said no kissing. At no point did I agree to keep my carnal thoughts to myself, nor will I ever agree to that. If I want to tell you that

I'm salivating to slide that dress off your shoulders and watch it fall to the ground as it bares your naked body, I will. I might even tell you that I taste you in my sleep sometimes and I wake up with a boner that I can't get rid of until I fantasize about you in the shower." Her cheeks flushed. From embarrassment at his dirty talk or guilt because she liked it? He couldn't tell. He leaned closer and whispered, "Believe it or not, I can tell you what I want to do to you without acting on it."

A car door slammed behind her and she recoiled as if it had been a gunshot to her torso.

"Invite me in," she muttered with a glance over her shoulder. "This is a party, isn't it?"

Should have been a party for two with a strict dress code—birthday suits only. Why had he agreed to her insane stipulation that they abstain from any kind of physical contact until the wedding? It was a dumb rule that made no sense and if Jonas and his wife, Viv, weren't waltzing up the front walk at that precise moment, Hendrix would be having a completely different conversation about it with his fiancée.

He stepped back and allowed Roz to enter, slipping an arm around her waist as she tried to flounce past him into the living room. "Oh, no you don't, sweetheart. Flip around and greet the guests. We're a couple."

Her smile grew pained as he drew her close. "How could I forget?"

Jonas and Viv hit the welcome mat holding hands. Funny how things worked. Jonas and Viv had gotten married in Vegas during the same trip where Hendrix had hooked up with Roz.

"Hey, guys. This is Roz," Hendrix announced unnecessarily, as he was pretty sure both Jonas and Viv knew who she was. If not from the photo flying around the internet, strictly by virtue of the fact that she was glued to his side.

Viv, bless her, smiled at Roz and shook her hand. "I'm Viv Kim. It's nice to meet you, and not just because I love any opportunity to use my new name."

With an intrigued expression, Roz glanced at the male half of the couple. "Are you newly married?"

Jonas stuck his hand out. "Brand-new. I'm Jonas Kim. My name is still the same."

Hendrix nearly rolled his eyes but checked it in deference to one of his oldest friends. "Thanks for coming. Roz and I are glad you're here to celebrate our engagement. Come in, please."

He guided them all to the cavernous living area that had been designed with this type of gathering in mind. The ten-thousand-square-foot house in Oakwood had been a purchase born out of a desire to stake his claim. There was a pride in ownership that this house delivered. It was a monument of a previous age, restored lovingly by someone with an eye for detail, and he appreciated the history wafting from its bones.

The house was a legitimate home and it was his.

Curiously, Viv's gaze cut between the two of them as she took a seat next to Jonas on the couch. "Have you set a wedding date?"

"Not yet," Roz answered and at the same time, Hendrix said, "Five weeks."

She shot him a withering look. "We're waiting until we pick a venue, which might dictate the date."

The doorbell rang and his mother arrived with Paul Carpenter right on her heels. Introductions all around went smoothly as nearly everyone knew each other. As the CEO of Kim Electronics, Jonas had met Mr. Carpenter several times at trade shows and various retail functions. Helene frequented Viv's cupcake shop on Jones Street apparently and exclaimed over the baker's wares at length. It was Paul and Helene's first meeting, however.

Hendrix raised a brow at the extra beat included in their hand shake, but forgot about it as Roz's friend Lora showed up with a date. Hendrix's other best friend, Warren Garinger, was flying solo tonight, which was lately his default. He arrived a pointed thirty minutes late.

It wasn't until later that evening that Hendrix had a chance to corner his friend on his tardiness.

"Just the man I was looking for," he said easily as he found Warren in the study examining one of the many watercolors the decorator had insisted went with the spirit of the house.

Warren pocketed his phone, which should have melted from overuse a long time ago. He worked ninety hours a week running the energy drink company his family had founded, but Hendrix didn't think that was what had put the frown on his friend's face. "I had to take a call. Sorry."

"The CEO never gets a day off," Hendrix acknowledged with a nod. "It's cool. I was just making sure you weren't hiding out in protest."

"I'm here, aren't I?" Warren smoothed out his expression before it turned into a full-bore scowl. "You've obviously made your decision to get married despite the pact."

Hendrix bit back a sigh. They'd been over this. Looked like they were going over it again. "The pact means something to me. And to Jonas. We're still tight, no matter what."

Jonas, Warren and Hendrix had met at Duke University, forming a friendship during a group project along with a fourth student, Marcus Powell. They'd had a lot of fun, raised a lot of hell together in the quintessential college experience—until Marcus had gotten his heart tangled up over a woman who didn't deserve his devotion. She'd been a traitorous witch of a cheerleader who liked toying with a man's affections more than she'd liked Marcus. Everyone had seen she was trouble. Except their friend.

He'd grown paler and more wasted away the longer she didn't give him the time of day and eventually, his broken heart had overruled his brain and somehow suicide had become his answer. Shell-shocked and embittered, the three surviving friends had vowed to never let a woman drive them to such lows. They'd formed a pact, refusing to fall in love under any circumstances.

Hell, that had been a given for Hendrix, pact or not. Love wasn't something he even thought much about because he never got close enough to a woman to develop any kind of tender feelings, let alone anything deeper.

But the pact—that was sacred. He'd had little in his life that made him feel like he belonged and his friendship with Jonas and Warren meant everything to him. He'd die before violating the terms of their agreement.

"If the pact is so important, then I don't understand why you'd risk breaking it with marriage," Warren countered and the bitterness lacing his tone sliced at Hendrix far more severely than he'd have expected.

They both glanced up as Jonas joined them, beers in hand. "Thought I'd find you two going at it if I looked hard enough. I'm the one you want to yell at, Warren. Not this joker."

Hendrix took the longneck from his friend's hand and gave Warren a pointed look until the other man sighed, accepting his own beer. No one was confused about the significance. It was a peace offering because Jonas had already broken the pact by falling in love with Viv. Warren had not taken it well. The three of them were still figuring out how to not be bachelor pals any longer, and how to not be at odds over what Warren viewed as Jonas's betrayal.

Hendrix just wanted everything to be on an even keel again so he didn't get a panicky feeling at the back of his throat when he thought of losing the one place where he felt fully accepted no matter what— inside the circle of his friends.

"If it makes you feel better," Hendrix said after a long swallow of his brew, "the odds of me falling in love with Roz are zero. We're not even sleeping together."

Jonas choked on his own beer. "Please. Is this April Fools' Day and I missed it?"

"No, really." Hendrix scowled as both his friends started laughing. "Why is that funny?"

"You've finally met the one woman you can't seduce and you're *marrying* her?" Warren clapped Hendrix on the back, still snickering.

"Shut up," he growled. Why did that have to be the one thing that got his buddy out of his snit? "Besides, I can go without sex."

"Right." Jonas drew the word out to about fourteen syllables, every one of them laden with sarcasm. "And I can pass as Norwegian."

Since Jonas was half-Korean, his point was clear. And Hendrix didn't appreciate his friend's doubt, never mind that he'd been angling for a way to kibosh the no-sex part of his agreement with Roz. "I don't have to explain myself to you guys."

Jonas sipped his beer thoughtfully. "Well, I guess it's a fair point that this is a fake marriage, so maybe you're pretty smart to skip sex in order to avoid confusion. I of all people can understand that."

"This marriage is not fake," Hendrix corrected. "*Your* marriage was fake because you're a moron who thought it was better to live together and just pretend you're hot and heavy. I'm not a moron. Roz and I will have a real marriage, with plenty of unfake hot and heavy."

Especially the honeymoon part. He was already glancing at travel websites for ideas on places he could take his bride where they'd have no interruptions during a weeklong smorgasbord where Roz was the only thing on the menu.

Jonas raised his eyebrows. "You're trying to tell me you're waiting until marriage before you sleep together? That's highly unconventional for anyone, let alone you."

It was on the tip of his tongue to remind Jonas how late Hendrix had been to his wedding. Roz had been the reason, and these yokels were lucky he'd showed up at all. It had been sheer hell to peel himself out of Roz's bed to make it to the chapel before the nuptials were over.

But something held him back from flinging his

escapades in his friends' faces. Maybe it had something to do with their assumption that he was a horn-
dog who couldn't keep it in his pants, which had
frankly been Roz's assumption, too. Was that all
there was to him in everyone's mind? Always on the
lookout for the next woman to nail? There was a lot
more complexity to his personality than that and he
was suddenly not thrilled to learn he'd overshadowed
his better qualities with his well-deserved reputation.

"That's me. Unconventional," he agreed easily.

And now he had an ironclad reason to stick to
his agreement…to prove to himself that he could
stay out of a woman's bed.

Roz's father had smiled at her tonight more times
than he had in the past five years. As much as she'd
craved his approval, all this cheer made her nervous. Paul Carpenter ran a billion-dollar furniture
enterprise, with manufacturing outlets and retail
stores under his command as far away as the Phil-
ippines and as close as within walking distance. He
rarely smiled, especially not at Roz.

"I've always liked this house," her father commented to her out of the blue as they found themselves at the small minibar at the same time.

"I think Hendrix mentioned it's on the Raleigh
Historical Society's list as one of the oldest homes
in Oakwood. It's really beautiful."

Small talk with her father about her fiancé's house.

It was nearly surreal. They didn't chat often, though that could be because she rarely gave him a chance. After years of conversations laden with her father's heavy sighs and pointed suggestions, she preferred their communication to be on a need-only basis.

Maybe that tide had turned. Hendrix, Jonas and Warren had disappeared, likely having a private no-girls-allowed toast somewhere away from the crowd, so there was no one to interrupt this nice moment.

"You haven't mentioned it, but I'd really like it if you allowed me to walk you down the aisle," her father suggested casually.

Something bright and beautiful bloomed in her chest as she stared at his aged but still handsome face. She'd never even considered having the kind of wedding where such a thing happened, largely because it had never occurred to her that he'd be open to the idea. They'd never been close, not even after her mother died. The experience of witnessing someone they both loved being eaten alive by cancer should have bonded them. For a long time, she let herself be angry that it hadn't. Then she'd started to wonder if he'd gotten so lost in his grief that he'd forgotten he had a daughter dealing with her own painful sense of loss.

Eventually, she sought to cauterize her grief in other ways, which had led to even further estrangement. Was it possible that she'd erased years of disappointment with the one simple act of agreeing to Hendrix's outrageous proposal?

"Of course." She swallowed a brief and unexpected tide of emotion. "That would be lovely."

Thankfully, her fiancé was already on board with planning an honest-to-God wedding with all the trimmings. She'd have to talk him into a longer engagement if they were going to have the type of wedding with an aisle, because she'd envisioned showing up at the justice of the peace in a Betsey Johnson dress that could support a corsage. The simpler the better.

But that was out the window. She had another agenda to achieve with her wedding now, and it included walking down an aisle on her father's arm. Dare she hope this could be a new beginning to their relationship?

"I wasn't sure you'd like the idea of me marrying Hendrix Harris," she said cautiously, trying to gauge how this new dynamic was supposed to work. She'd left a message to tell him about the party and its purpose, effectively announcing her engagement to her father via voice mail so he couldn't express yet more disappointment in her choices.

"I think it's great," he said with enthusiasm she'd rarely heard in his voice. "I'm happy that you're settling down. It will be good for you."

Keep her out of trouble, more like. It was in the undertone of his words and she chose not to let it sour the moment. She did have some questionable decisions in her rearview mirror or she wouldn't have needed to marry Hendrix in the first place. The fact that her dad liked the move was a plus she hadn't dared put on the list of pros, especially given that she was marrying a man her father and everyone else had seen in the buff.

"I think it will be good for me, too," she said, though her reasons were different than his.

"I did wonder if this wedding wasn't designed to eliminate the negative effects of that unfortunate photograph on Helene Harris's campaign." Her father sipped the scotch in a highball, deliberately creating a pregnant pause that prickled across the back of Roz's neck. "If so, that's a good move. Additionally, there are a lot of benefits to being the governor's daughter-in-law, and I like the idea of being tied to the Harris family through marriage."

That had not been a chance statement. "What, like maybe I could put in a good word for you?"

He nodded thoughtfully, oblivious to her sarcasm. "Something like that. I've had some thoughts about going into politics. This is an interesting development. Lots of opportunities unfolding as we speak."

She shouldn't be so shocked. But her stomach still managed to turn over as she absorbed the idea that her father only liked that she was marrying Hendrix because of how it benefited *him*. Did it not occur to her father that she didn't have any sort of in with Helene Harris yet? Geez. She'd only met the woman for the first time tonight. And Roz might only have a certain number of favor chips to cash in. The first item on her list was Ms. Harris in white face paint with big floppy shoes.

What was going to happen if she couldn't create the opportunity her father was looking for?

Everyone was expecting something from this union. Why that created such a bleak sense of disillusionment, she had no idea. It wasn't like she'd ever done anything else her father liked. It was just that for once, she'd thought they were finally forming a relationship.

Of course that wasn't the case. Fine. She was used to losing things, used to the temporary nature of everything good that had ever happened to her. It was just one more reason to keep everyone at arm's length.

But Hendrix made that vow harder to keep almost immediately, cornering her in the kitchen where she'd gone to lick her wounds.

"Studying up on my pots and pans so you can cook me a proper dinner once you're the little woman?" he asked as he sauntered into the room and skirted the wide marble-topped island that separated the sink from the 12-burner Viking range to join her on the far side.

"Unless you like your balls in your throat, I would refrain from ever referring to me as the little woman again," she informed him frostily, not budging an inch even as the big, solid wall of Hendrix's masculinity overwhelmed her. "Also, this is a private party. See yourself out."

He had some nerve, waltzing into her space without invitation. All it would take was one slight flex of her hips and they'd be touching. Hell, that might even happen if she breathed deeper.

Instead of getting huffy about her command, he just watched her, his eyes darkening. He was too close, smelled too much like a memory of sin and sex.

"What?" she asked testily as a long, sensual thread pulled at her center.

She swallowed a yelp as he snagged a lock of hair, tucking it behind her ear. But the touch was just an excuse to get even closer, of course, because once he had his hand on her, he didn't stop there. His thumb cruised down her jaw, sensitizing her entire face.

In some alternate dimension, there was a Rosalind Carpenter with the will to slap this man's hand away when he took liberties she hadn't invited. In this dimension, her stilettos had been cemented to the floor and she couldn't do anything but stand frozen as he tipped up her chin.

She braced for the crush of his lips on hers. Anticipated it. Leaned into it ever so slightly.

But then he shocked the hell out of her by tilt-

KAT CANTRELL   63

ing her head to the side and grazing her cheek as he murmured in her ear, "Wanna tell me what's got you so upset?"

Oh, no he didn't. How dare he make this about something other than sex and be dead on target about her reasons for hiding out at the same time?

"I'm not upset." Her pulse tripped all over itself, scrambling to sort his dominating presence from his uncanny ability to read her. "Maybe I like the kitchen."

And sure enough—with each breathy catch of her lungs—their bodies brushed and the contact sang through her.

"You can't snow the master of winter," he advised her so softly that she had to lean in a little closer to hear. Or at least that was her excuse and she'd cling to it as long as she could. "So lie to your friends, your dad. Anyone other than me. We're in this together and I need you."

Her knees went a little mushy. *Mushy*. The one person she had zero intention of letting under her skin had just demonstrated a remarkable ability to blaze right past every barrier she'd ever constructed. And it didn't even seem to matter that he hadn't meant those words the way they'd sounded, like he cared about her and had her back.

No. He wanted her to stick to the deal and stop being such a big baby about the fact that her father expected favors from this union. Weren't favors the whole purpose of this marriage? For God knew what reason, the fact that Hendrix had figured out all the subtle nuances of her mood hooked something inside her.

That pissed her off. He wasn't supposed to be good at handling her. He wasn't supposed to be anything but a means to an end.

"Yes," she purred and let her hips roll forward just a touch until she hit the thick, hard length she'd been seeking. "I can feel how much you need me."

"Careful." His lips feathered against her ear, sending shafts of need deep inside *her*. "Or I might think you're trying to entice me into breaking my promise. The Roz I know wouldn't play so dirty. So I'm going to assume it's a distraction from what's really going on with you and roll with it."

Before she could blink, his arm snaked around her waist, shoving her firmly into the cradle of his body, exactly where she wanted to be.

What did it say that he knew that about her too without being told?

"Put some of that sass where it belongs," he said into her ear as their embrace got a whole lot more intimate. He pressed her back against the counter, one leg teasing her thighs like he might push between them but he'd give her a minute to think about it. "Don't let a stray comment cramp your style. Be the life of the party because no one else's opinion matters."

Her eyes burned all at once. Oh, God, he was going to make her cry. What was wrong with her that a couple of compassionate phrases from a player like Hendrix could yank loose *tears*?

Except he wasn't just a creep looking to score. They were engaged, as unbelievable as that was to reconcile, and he needed her to *pull it together*.

"You're right," she admitted. "I'm letting crap that doesn't matter get me down."

What was she doing skulking around in the kitchen when there was a party going on? More importantly, he'd given her the perfect excuse to step out of his arms as everything settled inside.

She didn't move.

"Of course I am," he told her and she could hear the smile in his voice even as she absorbed his heat through her little black dress. "Roz, this is practice for the wider swath of society that we have to wade through an exhausting number of times over the next few weeks. They're not going to be any more forgiving. But I'm here. I'm not going anywhere and I'll be holding your hand the whole time."

"PB&J for the win," she murmured and dang it, her arms fit so well around his waist that she couldn't do anything but leave them there. "Although I have to ask why we couldn't have had this conversation without you wrapping yourself around me like an octopus."

"Oh, we could have." He nuzzled her ear. "This

was strictly for me. You're driving me insane in that dress and all I can think about is that I don't get to take it off at the end of the night. I deserve something for my suffering."

That shouldn't have made her laugh. Especially since the whole of his body pressed into hers felt more like the opening act than the finale.

"Also," he continued, "I didn't think you were in the mood for an audience. If anyone came through that door right now, they'd exit pretty quickly for fear of intruding on a moment between lovers."

Did the man ever miss an angle? She did not want to appreciate any of his qualities, let alone the nonsexual variety.

Neither should she be recalling with perfect clarity what he'd said to her on his front porch. He'd never been shy about using his mouth in whatever inventive way came to mind, and he had a really great imagination, especially when it came to talking dirty.

That was enough to jump-start her brain. This wasn't the start of a seduction, never mind how easily it could be. It was a Come to Jesus at the hands of her partner and she was the one who'd taken sex off the table. For a reason. The man made her forget her own name and she needed to keep her wits about her, or she'd never survive this. She had to get Clown-Around off the ground and Hendrix was nothing to her except a ticket to achieving her goals.

"The moment is over," she informed him through sheer force of will.

"I disagree." But he stepped back immediately, taking all his delicious heat with him.

Even in that, he'd read her expertly, extracting himself as soon as he sensed her consent had changed. His gaze burned hot and she had no doubt he'd sweep her back into his arms if she gave the word.

And that put the steel in her spine that had been missing. She had equal power in this partnership. He wasn't going to slip through her fingers when she wasn't looking because they weren't a couple basing their relationship on fleeting feelings. They both had goals, none of which would be accomplished when one of them moped around poking at old bruises.

Hendrix was a smart choice. Obviously. He got her in ways no one ever had and she refused to examine how much she liked that.

"We're a power couple." She held out her hand to him. "Let's go act like one."

Four

Hendrix nursed a Jack Daniel's on the rocks as he hung out near the fireplace on the east end of the house and wished like hell he could blame the whiskey for the burn in his throat. But that pain was pure Roz.

And maybe some leftover crap from the discussion with Jonas and Warren, where his so-called friends had made it known in no uncertain terms how weak they thought he was when it came to women.

He could go without sex. He could. Hadn't he walked away from Roz when she'd said walk? If that wasn't a stellar test of his iron will, he didn't know what was. And he'd passed.

So why was he still so pissed? His skin felt like

a hundred ants were crawling over it as he failed yet again at keeping his eyes off his fiancée. She lit up the room as she talked to his mother. So what if anyone caught him staring? He and Roz were engaged and he was allowed to look at her. In fact, he'd say it was expected.

The unexpected part was how…fierce the whole encounter in the kitchen had made him. Someone had upset Roz and he didn't like it. Didn't like how fragile she'd felt in his arms as he did his best to beat back whatever was going on with her internally. But she'd snapped out of it like the champ she was and he'd had a hard time letting her go when what he really wanted to do was explore that lush mouth of hers. That wasn't what she'd needed. Wasn't what he needed, either.

Okay, it was what he *needed* all right. But he also needed to prove to everyone—and maybe to himself—that he had what it took to reel back his sex-soaked lifestyle. If he'd learned to do that when his mother had asked him to, Vegas wouldn't have happened and there'd be no photograph of Hendrix's bare butt plastered all over the internet.

Paul Carpenter loomed in Hendrix's peripheral vision and then the man parked near him with a lift of his glass. "Haven't had a chance to speak to you one-on-one yet."

"No, sir."

Hendrix eyed the older man whose wealth and

power in the retail industry eclipsed almost everyone in the world. Certainly a smaller chain like Harris Tobacco Lounge had nothing on Carpenter Furniture, nor did people get vaguely distasteful looks on their faces when talking about the business Roz's father had founded. Tobacco wasn't in vogue any longer, not the way it had been in the late eighties when Helene had partnered with her brother to build a string of shops from the ground up. Hendrix had joined the company almost a year after Uncle Peter died and then worked ninety hours a week to pull miracle after miracle from thin air to increase revenue over the past decade as he gradually took over the reins from his mom.

But Hendrix didn't assume for a moment that a man like Paul Carpenter respected one thin dime of Harris tobacco money, regardless of how hard he and his mom had worked for their fortune.

Mr. Carpenter eyed Hendrix as he swished his own amber liquid around the ice in his highball. "I suppose soon enough you'll be my son-in-law."

"Yes, sir." Why did it feel like he'd been called to the principal's office? He'd bet every last dollar of Harris money that Carpenter didn't think Hendrix was good enough for his daughter. "Roz is pretty important to me."

Uncomfortable didn't begin to describe this conversation. Hendrix shifted his stance. Didn't help.

"She's important to me, too," Paul said with a

small smile. "It's just been the two of us since she was eight, you know."

"Yes, she mentioned that her mother had passed away." It was something they had in common—a missing parent. But Carpenter hadn't thrown that tidbit in for anything close to the same reason as Roz had. At the time, they'd been playing truth or dare and doing Jell-O shots off each other's bare stomachs. "I'm sorry for your loss, sir."

The memory of Roz's hot body decked out on the bed with the little circle of raspberry gelatin covering her navel slammed through his senses with far more potency than he'd have expected given that he'd just had the woman in his arms less than fifteen minutes ago.

Problem was that she'd been dressed. And off-limits. And probably even if he'd had permission to boost her up on the counter so he could get underneath that black dress, he'd still want her with a bone-deep ache. That had happened in Vegas, too. He couldn't get enough of her skin, her abandon, the way she was always game for whatever he did next.

And that was a conviction of his crimes as much as anything else. He had few memories of Roz that didn't involve her naked. That was the way he liked it…and lent entirely too much credence to everyone's certainty that he was a walking boner, panting after the next piece of tail he could get his hands on.

God, what was wrong with him? He was having

a conversation with his future father-in-law and all
he could think about was casting the man's daughter in the dirtiest sex scenario imaginable.

Something that might have been a blush if he'd
been a girl prickled across his cheeks. But embarrassment wasn't something he did. Ever. He had
nothing to be ashamed of. Except for the handful
of scandals he'd managed to fall into over the past
few years—Roz had certainly not been the first. She
was just the one that had been the most worth it.

He sighed as Paul nodded his thanks over Hendrix's condolences. Maybe if he thought about
something else, like cars, he could pretend the hard-
on he'd been carrying around since Roz walked
through his front door would eventually go away.

"I'm not one to pry," Paul said in that tone people
used when they meant the exact opposite of what
they'd just claimed. "And it's none of my business.
But I wanted you to know that if you're marrying
Roz to eliminate the scandal, I approve."

"You, um…what?" Hendrix swallowed. It didn't
work. Throat still burned. He gulped enough whiskey to choke a horse, coughed and then had to wipe
his watering eyes.

Paul Carpenter *approved* of Hendrix's marriage
to Roz. As if Hendrix was someone he might have
picked out for his daughter. It was as shocking as
it was unbelievable.

For the first time in his life, he'd been automatically accepted by a male of note, one he wasn't related to, whom he admired, one whose approval he would have never sought, save this specific situation. And he'd *never* expected to get it.

"It's high time that Roz take responsibility for the questionable decisions she makes, especially the one that led to so much trouble for you and your mother's campaign. I appreciate that you've been a willing party to the *fix*." Paul accompanied that word with two fingered air quotes.

The elation that had accompanied the man's initial statement fizzled. Fast.

A willing party? As if Roz had somehow seduced him into indulging a one night stand and then orchestrated the photograph? As if Hendrix had been an innocent victim of her stupidity?

Agape and unable to actually close his mouth around the sour taste coating his tongue, Hendrix let Paul's meaning filter through his brain for a good long while. At least until he felt like he could respond without punching Paul in the mouth.

"It takes two to tango. Sir." Hendrix lifted his chin. "Roz and I are partners. I'm making all my own decisions and rest assured, one of them is to treat her like the amazing, wonderful woman that she is."

He stopped short of telling Paul that he should take a lesson.

Figured the one time he'd had a few moments of approval from a man who could have been a father figure would end in the realization that Roz hadn't had a relationship with her surviving parent the way Hendrix had. Hendrix's mother loved him and while his exploits exasperated her, she never judged. Not the way this sanctimonious jerk had just judged Roz.

Roz was Paul's daughter and he should be on her side. If anything, Hendrix had been expecting a talking-to about corrupting the Carpenter daughter with his evil ways, which would have been well-deserved and easy to pretend didn't affect him. Instead, he felt like he needed to take a shower and then tuck Roz away where this man couldn't touch her.

"Well, be that as it may, I for one am quite happy with the development. Marriage will be good for Roz and with any luck, she'll stop the naked romps in hot tubs."

"Sir, I mean this with all due respect, but I sincerely hope not."

Hendrix whirled and left Paul standing by the fireplace with a bemused look on his face. Having an in with Carpenter Furniture wasn't going to pave the way to belonging in the upper echelon of North Carolina businessmen then. But what *would* make Hendrix finally feel like he was legitimate?

He found Roz talking to Lora in his study and took only half a second to gauge Roz's mood. Better. She didn't seem fragile any longer. Good. He grabbed his fiancée's hand, threw an apologetic glance at her friend and dragged Roz from the room.

"What are you doing?" she demanded once they hit the hall.

"You and I are going to go do something together. And we'll be dressed."

Then he'd have a memory of her that had nothing to do with sex. They both needed that.

"Darling, we *are* doing something together. Dressed." And Roz's sarcasm wasn't even as thick as it should be. "We're at our engagement party, remember?"

"Of course I do," he grumbled. A lie. He'd forgotten that he couldn't just leave and take Roz on an honest-to-God date.

Soon. It was an oversight that he'd beat himself up for later. He and Roz would—and *should*—go on lots of dates with each other while they weren't having sex. Spend time together. Get to know each other. Then he could stop thinking about her naked forty-seven times a minute.

But one thing he *couldn't* stop thinking about was the fact that he'd never have realized she was upset earlier if he'd been permitted to turn it into a sexual encounter. What else had he already missed because his interactions with his fiancée started and ended with how best to get into her panties? That question put a hollow feeling in his chest that stayed with him the rest of the night.

* * *

Roz took a long shower when she got home from the engagement party, hoping it would wash the evening from her brain. But nothing could dislodge the surprising things she'd learned about Hendrix in the course of a few hours. The man never did what she expected. But she'd already known *that*.

What she hadn't known was how easily he'd figure out how to bend her to his will. She'd naively assumed that as long as they weren't naked, she'd be good. Wrong. Somehow, he'd gotten her to agree to a date.

A date with Hendrix Harris. That was almost more unbelievable than the fact that she was marrying him. Yeah, their "date" was a public spectacle that he'd dreamed up as a way to push their agenda. Couldn't get society used to the idea that they were a respectable couple if they hid at home. She got that.

But for the love of God… What were they going to talk about? She didn't date. She had a lot of sex with men who knew their way around a woman's body but conversation by candlelight in an intimate booth at a swanky restaurant wasn't in her repertoire—by design. One she could handle; the other she could not. Intimacy born of conversation and dating led to feelings she had no intention of developing, so she avoided all of the above like the plague.

One surefire way to ensure a man never called

you again? Sleep with him. Worked every time. Unless his name was Hendrix Harris, apparently. That guy she couldn't figure out how to shake, mentally or physically.

At least the concept of going on a date with her fiancé had pushed the unpleasantness of the encounter with her father to the background. Actually, Hendrix had almost single-handedly done that with his comfort-slash-seduction scene in the kitchen, which she'd appreciated more than she'd ever let on.

The less the man guessed how much he affected her, the better.

The next morning, she rifled through her closet for something appropriate for a date with the man who'd blown through half the female population of Raleigh. All eyes would be on her and not for the normal reasons.

Nothing. How was it possible not to have a thing to wear in an entire eight-hundred-square-foot closet? She'd have to go shopping after she got some work done.

Donning a severe suit that she secretly called her Grown-up Outfit, she twisted her hair into a sleek up-do that made her feel professional and drove to Clown-Around to push some paperwork across her desk.

Her phone rang and she almost didn't answer the call from an unfamiliar number. It was too early and she hadn't had nearly enough coffee to endure more rejection from yet another hospital.

But she was the only one here. There was no one else to do the dirty work. She answered.

"Rosalind?" the female voice said. "This is Helene Harris. How are you?"

Roz nearly dropped the phone but bobbled it just enough to keep it near her face. "Ms. Harris. I'm fine. Thank you. It was lovely to meet you last night."

"Likewise. I hope you don't mind that I asked Hendrix for your number. I'd like to take you to lunch, if you're free."

"I'm free." That had probably come out a little too eagerly. Thank you, Jesus, she'd worn an outfit that even a future mother-in-law would approve of. "And thank you. That would be lovely."

They made plans to meet at a restaurant on Glenwood Avenue, dashing Roz's notion to go shopping for a date dress, but she couldn't think about that because *holy crap*—she was having lunch with her future mother-in-law, who was also running for governor and who had presumably agreed to be a clown. Plus there was a whole mess of other things running through her head and now she was nervous.

By lunchtime, Roz truly thought she might throw up. That would put the cap on her day nicely, wouldn't it? A photo of her yakking all over a gubernatorial candidate would pair well with the one of her *in flagrante delicto* with the woman's son.

Ms. Harris had beaten her to the restaurant and was waiting for Roz near the maître d' stand, looking polished, dignified and every inch a woman who could run a state with one hand tied behind her back. In other words, not someone Roz normally hung around with.

"Am I late?" she asked Ms. Harris by way of greeting. Because that was a great thing to point out if so.

Ms. Harris laughed. "Not at all. I got here early so I didn't have to make you wait."

"Oh. Well, that was nice. Thank you." A little floored, Roz followed the older woman to a table near the window that the maître d' pointed them to.

The murmur of voices went into free fall as the two ladies passed. Heads swiveled. Eyes cut toward them. But unlike what had happened to Roz the last time she'd braved polite society, the diner's faces didn't then screw up in distaste as they recognized her. Instead, the world kept turning and people went back to eating as if nothing had happened.

Miraculous.

Roz slid into her chair and opened her menu in case she needed something to hide behind. Ms. Harris didn't do the same. She folded her hands on the table and focused on Roz with a sunny smile that reminded her of Hendrix all at once.

"I'm so jealous that you can wear your hair up," Ms. Harris said out of the blue and flicked a hand at her shoulder-length ash-blond hair. "I can't. I look like a Muppet. But you're gorgeous either way."

"Um…thank you," Roz spit out because she had to say something, though it felt like she was repeating herself. "Ms. Harris, if I may be blunt, I need some context for this lunch. Are we here so you can tell me to lie low for the foreseeable future? Because I'm—"

"Helene, please." She held up a hand, palm out in protest, shooting Roz a pained smile. "Ms. Harris is running for governor and I hear that enough all day long. I like to leave her at the office."

"Helene, then." Roz blinked. And now she was all off-kilter. Or rather more so than she'd been since the woman had called earlier that morning. Come to think of it, she'd been upside down and inside out since the moment she'd caught Hendrix's eye at the Calypso Room. Why would lunch with his mother be any different? "I'm sorry. Call me Roz. Rosalind is an old-fashioned name that would be better suited for an eighty-year-old woman who never wears pants and gums her food."

Fortunately, Helene laughed instead of sniffing and finding something fascinating about the tablecloth the way most polished women did when confronted with Roz's offbeat sense of humor. She hadn't grown up going to cotillions and sweet-sixteen balls the way other girls in her class had, and her lack of decorum showed up at the worst times. Her father had been too busy ignoring the fact that he had a daughter to notice that she preferred sneaking out and meeting twenty-year-old boys with motorcycles to dances and finishing school.

"I think it's a beautiful name. But I get that we can't always see our own names objectively. If I had a dime for every person who called me Helen." She made a tsk noise and waved away the waiter who was hovering near her elbow. "And then try to give your own kid an unusual name that no one on the planet can mispronounce and all you get is grief."

In spite of herself, Roz couldn't help but ask. "Hendrix doesn't like his name? Why not?"

Helene shrugged and shook her head, her discreet diamond earrings catching the low light hanging over the table. "He says Hendrix was a hack who would have faded by the time he reached thirty if he hadn't overdosed. Blasphemy. The man was a legend. You'd think your fiancé would appreciate being named after a guitar hero, but no."

"He…he thinks Jimi Hendrix is a *hack*?" Roz clutched her chest, mock-heart-attack style, mostly to play along because she knew who the guitarist was of course, but she had no opinion about his status as a legend. Neither had she been born yesterday. You didn't argue musical taste with the woman who would most likely be sitting in the governor's chair after the election. "I might have to rethink this whole wedding idea."

The other woman grinned wide enough to stick a salad plate in her mouth sideways. "I knew I liked you." Helene evaluated Roz for a moment and then signaled the waiter. "As much as I'd prefer to spend the rest of the afternoon hanging out, duty calls. We should eat."

Since it sounded like a mandate, Roz nodded, trying to relax as Helene ordered a salad and water. This wasn't the Spanish Inquisition that she'd expected, not yet anyway. Maybe that was coming after lunch. She ordered a salad despite loathing them because it was easy to eat and obviously an approved dish since Helene had gotten the same.

And that was the root cause of her nervousness—she wanted Helene to like her but had no clue how to go about that when she had no practice cozying up to a motherly type. Furthermore, the woman had just said she liked her. What more did Roz need in the way of validation, a parade?

She sipped her water and yearned for a glass of wine, which would be highly inappropriate. Wouldn't it?

"Thank you," Helene murmured to her after the waiter disappeared. "For agreeing to this wedding plan that we came up with. It speaks a lot of your character that you'd be willing to do something so unconventional to help me."

"I…" *Have no idea how to respond to that.* Roz sat back in her chair and resisted the urge to rub at her temples, which would only clue in everybody that she'd fallen completely out of the rhythm of the conversation. "I— You're welcome?"

Smiling, Helene patted Roz's hand, which was currently clenched in a fist on the tablecloth. "Another thing. You're making me nervous, dear. I can't decide if you're about to bolt or dissolve into tears. I asked you to lunch because I want to get to know you. You're the only daughter I've ever had. For as long as I've got you, let's make this a thing, shall we?"

Unexpected tears pricked at Roz's eyelids, dang it. The Harris family shared that gene apparently— Hendrix had that uncanny ability to pull stuff out of her depths, too.

"I don't have a mother," she blurted out. "So this is all new to me."

Helene nodded. "I understand that. I didn't have a good relationship with my mother. Sometimes growing up, I wondered if it would have been easier if she'd disowned me instead of spending every waking second being disappointed in me."

Roz nodded, mortified as she dashed tears away with the white napkin from her lap. This was not the conversation she'd intended to have with her new mother-in-law. She didn't believe for a second that shouting, *I still wonder that about my father!*

would be the best way to foster the relationship Helene seemed to be asking for.

But Helene's story so closely mirrored the way Roz felt about her father that it was uncanny. How familiar was she allowed to be on her first one-on-one with Helene? This was uncharted—and so not what she'd expected. If anything, she'd earned an indictment for playing a role in the problems that Helene had just thanked her for helping to solve. There'd been two naked people in that hot tub, after all.

"I'm sorry about the photograph," she said earnestly and only because Helene hadn't called her on the carpet about it. That was why Roz and her father were always at such odds. He always adopted that stern tone when laying out Roz's sins that immediately put her back up.

Accepting the apology with a nod, Helene waited for the server to put their salads on the table and leaned forward. "Trust me when I tell you that we all have questionable exploits in our pasts. You just got lucky enough for yours to be immortalized forever, which frankly wouldn't have happened if you'd been with anyone other than Hendrix."

That was entirely false. Bad luck of the male variety followed her around like a stray dog, waiting to turn its canines on her the moment she tried to feed it. Roz swallowed and ate a tiny bit of salad in order not to seem ungrateful. "I have a tendency to get a little, um, enthusiastic with my exploits un-fortunately."

"Which is no one's business but yours. The un-fortunate part is that my son forgot that political enemies have long reaches and few scruples. You can only tell the kid so much. He does his own thing." She shrugged good-naturedly, far more so than should have been the case. It was a testament to Helene's grace, which was something Roz had no experience with.

"You're very generous," Roz said with a small frown that she couldn't quite erase. "Most parents aren't so forgiving."

At least that had never been Roz's experience. Parents were harsh, not understanding.

"I'm not most parents. Hendrix is my life and I love him more than I could possibly tell you. He saved me." Helene paused to eat some of her own salad but Roz didn't dare interrupt. "I have a bit of a wild past myself, you know."

Was this the part where Roz was supposed to nod and say, *Why yes, I have heard all the gossip about your rebellious teenage years*? Especially when Roz's own rebellious teenage years had been nothing but practice for her even more defiant twen-ties, when she'd really tested the limits of her fa-ther's patience.

"Getting pregnant at seventeen was a huge wake-up call," Helene recounted in the pause. "Without that baby, I might have continued in a self-destructive cycle that wouldn't have ended well. And now look at me. I created a successful business that Hendrix runs like the maestro of the boardroom that he was born to be and I'm running for governor. *Governor.* Some days, I don't know what I did to earn these blessings."

Roz's own eyes misted in commiseration as Helene dabbed at hers with her napkin. "I honestly wasn't sure what to think when you asked me to lunch. But making each other cry wasn't even on the top ten."

Helene's smile widened. One thing Roz noticed, no matter what, the woman's smile never slipped. It was a trait she'd like to learn because not for one moment did Roz believe that Helene's life was all smooth sailing. No, instead, Helene had some innate quality that allowed her to be happy regardless of the subject or circumstance. Voters must really be drawn to that happiness the same way Roz was.

Of course that apple did not fall far from the tree. Hendrix's bright personality had been a huge turn-on. Still was. He just laced it with pure carnal intentions that he did not mind making her fully aware of, and then followed through like the maestro of the *bedroom* that he was.

Roz shivered and tried like hell to reel back those thoughts because fantasizing about a woman's son while sitting with her in an upscale restaurant felt like bad form.

"I didn't plan to make you cry when I called you," Helene confessed sunnily. "Just happened. But I love that you're a companionable crier. No one wants to cry alone."

No. No one did. But that was some people's lot in life and if they didn't change the subject, there were going to be a lot more tears. The raw place inside was growing a lot bigger the longer she sat here. This wonderful woman had just said she'd be happy having a mother-daughter relationship with Roz for as long as Roz was married to Hendrix. Like that was an invitation Roz got every day and it was no big thing.

It was. And Roz wanted to cling to it, hold it and wrap her arms around it. But like everything—*everything*—in her life, Helene would be gone one day soon. Too soon. Any day was too soon because Roz had just realized that she craved whatever relationship this woman would grant her. Helene could be a…mentor of sorts. A friend. A stand-in mother.

It was overwhelming to contemplate. Overwhelmingly sad to think about having that and then giving it up.

But how could Roz refuse? She didn't *want* to refuse.

Helene was helping her blow away the scandal if nothing else and Roz owed the woman respect and allegiance for that alone.

The rest was all a huge bonus.

Five

Hendrix picked Roz up at the door of her loft for their date because he wanted to and he could. Also? What better way to prove he had all the skill necessary to resist pushing his way inside and having his way with her than not to do it?

But when he knocked on the door, she swung it wide to give him an eyeful of soft, gorgeous skin on display. Being that edible should be a crime. Her cleavage should be framed and hung on the wall of the Louvre.

"What happened to your pants?" he growled hoarsely.

Roz glanced down at the river of bare legs flowing from the hem of the blouse-like thing she had on. "What pants? This is a dress."

"The hell you say." He couldn't take her on a date in that outfit. His will would slide into the toilet in about a microsecond. Surely that would be the easiest dress in the history of time to get his hands under, even if they were someplace normally reserved for hands off, like a high-backed booth in the corner of a dimly lit restaurant.

His will made a nice whooshing sound as it flushed away and all his good intentions crumbled into dust. He might have whimpered.

Do not step over the threshold. Do not. No stepping.

"Let me make this perfectly clear to you," he ground out. "If you wear that dress—and I use that term *very* loosely—I cannot be responsible for what carnal activities may befall you in the course of this evening."

"Please." She waved that off. "You made a promise to keep your hands off me and you will, I have no doubt. What you're really saying is that you'd be embarrassed to be seen with me in this, right? So kiss off. I'm wearing it."

Oh, so it was going to be one of those nights. Not only would he have to contend with the idea that she had absolute faith in him, but she'd also assigned some kind of nefarious intent to his comments.

Her attitude needed to go and fast. "I wasn't embarrassed to be seen with you naked in a photograph. Not embarrassed now. Stop projecting your own crap all over me and get your purse. If you want to wear something that's one stiff breeze away from being illegal, be my guest."

"What's with you?" she called over her shoulder as she did exactly as he'd commanded without seeming to realize it. "You asked me on this date. If you're going to be nasty to me the whole time, then I'd be happy to slam the door in your face and order takeout."

That wasn't happening. He'd been looking forward to this date all day. "Why is it so hard to believe my objection to that dress starts and ends with how spectacular you look in it? You tell me what's with you and I'll tell you what's with me."

She smirked and flounced past him to the building's elevator. "You never had a problem with what I wore in Vegas. What's changed now? Only that we're engaged and you want me to look like a proper Harris bride."

Whatever *that* meant.

"Stop putting words in my mouth." The elevator door closed around them and they were alone in a space that got a whole lot smaller the more of her scent he breathed in. "In Vegas, I didn't care what you wore because I was taking it off you at some point. That's not the situation tonight and if you're really confused about the state of my extreme sexual frustration, the evidence is ready and available for your hands-on examination."

Her gaze flicked to his crotch, which put a little more heat into his already painful erection. Her sweet fingers on it would be legendary indeed but she didn't take him up on the invitation. Shame.

"I— You know what? Never mind." Her lush pink lips clamped together and she looked away.

Not so fast. His beleaguered senses were still working well enough to alert him that there was more here that he didn't know. "Spit it out, sweetheart. Or I'll be forced to kiss it out of you."

"What?" She slid him a sideways glance. "There's no stipulation in the rules that says you're allowed to kiss me to get information."

He shrugged. "How come you get to make all the rules? If you're not going to be honest with me, I have to make up my own rules."

Her sigh worked its way through his gut and he was a half second away from sweeping her into his arms to show her he always put his money where his mouth was. But then she did as he suggested.

"I am projecting," she admitted.

It was as much of a shock now as it had been in the kitchen during their party—he'd figured out how to make progress with Roz. She was such a mystery, one he'd like to spend many long hours solving. Usually he would do that in bed. But that was off-limits here, so he'd been forced to be more creative. Looked like it was working. "Don't do that. Tell me what's up and then we'll go paint the town."

"Maybe you want a wife more like your mom. Smart and accomplished." She shrugged, her face blank. "That's not who I am. I have to be me, even if I don't look like I'm supposed to be here."

"What does that even mean? Of course you're supposed to be here. What, are you worried how you stack up?" The long, intense silence answered his flippant question in spades. "Are you *kidding* me? That's really something that even crossed your mind?"

Ridiculous. But apparently it wasn't to her. She rolled her shoulders back and her spine went stiff.

"Can we just forget about it?"

That wasn't happening any more than not taking Roz on this date. But first they obviously needed to get a few things straight. The elevator reached the ground floor and he waited until she reached his car.

Instead of opening the door for her, he snagged her by the waist and turned her into his arms, trapping her against the car. Instantly, everything but Roz drained from his mind as her body aligned with his so neatly that he could feel the heat of her core against his leg.

That was some dress.

"I already told you what you wanted to know, Hendrix." She glanced up at him through her lashes and the look was so sexy it put at least an inch on his already impossibly hard erection. "What are you going to do now, kiss me anyway?"

"No need." His hips fit so well into the hollow of her stomach that he swayed into her a little deeper. "This is strictly Exhibit A. B and C will have to wait."

Because he'd given his word. How had that become such a thing? Fine time for something like principles. Before Roz, he'd have said he had none when it came to women. Or rather, women said that on his behalf and he'd never corrected the notion.

"Make no mistake, though. You need kissing," he murmured, ignoring the fact that it was so backward it wasn't even funny. "In the worst way. Anytime you find yourself worried about whether you're the most gorgeous woman in the room, you think about this. Remember what my body feels like against yours and don't you dare question whether you're the woman I want to take home with me."

"I wasn't worried about that," she said and blinked her long sooty lashes coquettishly. "But I do appreciate exhibit A."

Not enough to lift the no-kissing moratorium apparently. She was crushed against his body, wearing a filmy, flirty dress that barely covered her good parts and her lips came together in the sweetest little bow that he wanted to taste so badly he feared for his sanity.

But not enough that he'd lost all decorum.

Looked like his will wasn't completely broken because he found the wherewithal to step back. His chest heaved as he met her gaze. It was enigmatic and full of heat.

"Let me know when you're ready for the rest of the exhibit. I can open it up for your viewing pleasure any time."

Why were they torturing themselves like this again?

Due punishment, he reminded himself. His mom deserved to have a campaign free from other people's darts because of her son's actions. He owed it to his mother to fix it, especially after already messing up once because he couldn't resist this woman.

Plus, marrying Roz and introducing something real and legitimate into his life meant something to him, more than he'd ever admit, to her or anyone.

He tucked his fiancée into the car and slid into his own seat. She leaned on the center console instead of settling back against the leather, spilling way too much of her presence into his space.

"This seat has plenty of room for two," he murmured instead of starting the engine like a good boy.

"Don't threaten me unless you plan to follow through," she shot back and tucked her chin into her palm as if she planned to watch him the entire time he drove. "Where are you taking me? Not Randolph Room. That's where your mom took me to lunch."

"You had lunch with my mom?" That was news to him. He frowned.

Had his mother mentioned something about it last night and he'd forgotten in all the hoopla of the engagement party and the disturbing conversation with Paul Carpenter? He distinctly recalled giving Roz's number to his mom, but he'd assumed that was so they could coordinate the clown thing.

His mother usually told him her schedule and it was bothersome that she hadn't given him a heads-up about having lunch with his fiancée. He and Helene were business partners, and Hendrix sometimes offered advice on her campaign. And they were friends, which was often weird to people so he seldom talked about it.

Of course, since the photograph, she'd been a little on edge with him. It stung to find out they weren't totally back to normal.

"Yeah. She called me and asked if I was free. I wasn't going to say no."

"You shouldn't have. What did you talk about?"

"Girl stuff."

That was code for *mind your own business*. Hendrix started the car to give himself something to do that wasn't prying into the social life of his mother and fiancée. Nor did he want to obsess over the reasons why it was bothering him.

At least now he had some context for why Roz had all of a sudden joined the Helene Harris fan club and developed a complex about whether she stacked up against other women.

They drove to the restaurant where he'd made reservations and he cursed the silence that had fallen inside the car. Normally he had no problem finding something to talk about, particularly when it came to Roz, but he didn't want to spend the evening discussing all the ways he planned to have her after the wedding.

Well, he *wanted* to. There was absolutely nothing wrong with a healthy attraction to the woman you were going to marry. But he genuinely didn't think he had it in him to talk dirty to Roz and then not follow through yet again.

"Did you and my mother work out the clown stuff?" That was a safe enough subject.

"No. I mean, she mentioned it, but only to say that she's overcommitted right now and to bug her about it at lunch next week so she can fit it in. She actually said it like that. *Bug* her." Roz laughed. "As if I'd pester Helene like that. 'Mom, Mom, can you be a clown? Pleeeeease?'"

Hendrix did a double take at Roz's cute little girl voice. And the mention of additional lunches. "You're having lunch again?"

"Sure, we decided it was important to have a standing lunch date once a week from now on. Is there a problem with that?"

Yes. A huge problem. He didn't like the idea of

his mom getting chummy with Roz. Why? How the hell should he know? He just…didn't. "Of course not. I was making conversation. This is a date. The whole point is to get to know each other, right?"

"That was how you posed it," she reminded him with another laugh that should have had him thinking of all the ways he could get her to do that a lot because it meant she was having fun.

Instead, his back was up and his mood had slid into a place normally reserved for tense board meetings. What was *wrong* with him? Not enough sex lately, most likely.

At the restaurant, they waited in a discreet corner as the maître d' readied their table, both of them ignoring the pointed attention from the other guests. At least Roz hadn't stiffened up like she had at the florist. He'd consider that a win.

Wedding plans. That was a good subject. Surely they could talk about that. He waited until they'd both taken their seats and he'd given the waiter their wine preference.

"So. You're going to hang out with my mom once a week now?"

She lifted a brow. "That's really bothering you, isn't it?"

Apparently. And now it was evident to them both. He bit back a curse.

When was the last time his mom had asked him to lunch? Ages ago. Not since the photograph had hit the news. She'd been really upset. But it had all blown over after he'd agreed to marry Roz—he'd thought.

And look, here he was in a restaurant with Roz. Engaged. That had been a major feat to pull off. People were noticing them together and a waiter had even taken a discreet picture with his phone that would likely make the rounds with some positive press attached. Surely Helene could appreciate all of the steps Hendrix had taken toward legitimizing his relationship with Roz so that his mom's political opponents wouldn't have any fodder to lob at her via the press.

Now would be a great time to stop sulking and get back to the reason he was torturing himself with a stunning companion whom he would not be taking to bed later. They hadn't even scored a dimly lit booth, which was good. And bad.

"This is the part where you're supposed to back me into the kitchen and stick your hands all over my body so I can have something else to focus on besides the stuff in my head," he informed her.

"I would if that would help." She eyed him nonchalantly. "But I'm pretty sure that only works on me. Instead, why don't you tell me why you're so threatened by the idea of me having lunch with your mom?"

Lazily, he sipped his wine to cover the panic that

had uncurled in his stomach. The alcohol didn't help. "*Threatened* is a strong word."

And so correct. How dare she be the one to figure that out when he hadn't? The back of his neck flashed hot. That was a big wake-up call.

He'd never in a million years expected that getting married would mean he'd have to share his mother with someone. It had been the two of them for so long, and they'd become even more of a unit as he'd grown into adulthood, made even stronger after Uncle Peter had died. His reaction was pure selfishness and he didn't feel like apologizing for it all at once.

"Then you tell me what would be a better word," she said.

No quarter. If he wasn't already feeling pushed against a wall, her cool insistence would have put him there. *"Curious."*

Her small smile said she had his number and she'd be perfectly within her rights to call him on his complete lie. *Pissed off* and *tense* would be more applicable. Which was dumb. What, was he actually worried that Roz was going to steal his mother from him?

"Curious about why on earth two women who don't know each other and will soon share the same last name could possibly want to have lunch?" She watched him over the rim of her glass as she sipped her own wine.

"You're changing your name?" This evening was full of revelations.

"Yeah. Why not? That's part of the deal here, right? Marrying you is my get-out-of-jail-free card. Might as well go full throttle. Make sure everyone is clear that I'm tied to the governor's office."

"But you're already a Carpenter—" All at once, the conversation with her father slammed through his consciousness. Was he really that dense? Maybe being a Carpenter wasn't all that great for her. After being treated to a glimpse of the judgment levied in her direction, it wasn't so hard to guess why, if so. Maybe she deserved a name change.

Wow. When had he turned into such an ass?

He picked up her hand to hold it in his. Her touch bled through him, convicting him even further since she didn't pull away. "I shouldn't be jumping down your throat about having lunch with my mom. It's fine. I'm glad you're getting along."

She nodded and the mood lightened. The restaurant he'd selected featured a highly rated chef and the meal reflected that. They ate and conversed about innocuous subjects and he relaxed about halfway through dinner.

It wasn't until he escorted Roz to the valet stand that he realized the tension hadn't completely fled on her side. Her back felt stiff under his fingers. Okay, he'd royally screwed up earlier if she was still uptight over the third degree he'd given her. But why had she dropped it like everything was fine? Just like a woman to nurse a grudge and not bother to say anything about it. That wasn't going to fly.

As he pointed the car in the direction of her loft, he glanced at her from the corner of his eye. "Silent treatment for my crimes?"

She stared out the window. "Don't be ridiculous. I don't play little-girl games with men."

He let that simmer for a few minutes as he put a tight rein on his temper before he did something like comment on big-girl games. Nothing in his experience had prepared him to do this kind of long-term thing with a woman. And they were *getting married*. For the first time, it occurred to him that maybe he wasn't marriage material, that the reason he'd shied away from relationships wasn't solely because of the pact he'd made with Warren and Jonas, but also because he sucked at navigating emotional land mines.

But like the promise he'd made to keep his hands off her, this conversation was just as much a measure of his character. It was worth it to him to figure this out, if for no other reason than to prove he could.

He pulled over into a shadowy parking lot and killed the engine, then turned to face her. "Talk to me, Roz. You're obviously still upset."

"You asked me on a date so we could get to know each other. But then when you had an opportunity to really lay it all out, you didn't. At least have the courtesy to be honest with me. You don't like me being friendly with your mom because I'm just a good-time girl you had to marry because we got caught up in a scandal. I'm not good enough to be a real wife."

He shut his eyes for a blink, as that barb arrowed through his gut nice and deep. He had no excuse for not having seen that coming. Obviously she was playing back things she'd heard from others, and he'd unwittingly stepped right in the center of the land mines.

Yep. Not marriage material. This was why he stuck to sex, which he was good at, and shied away from anything that smacked of intimacy, which he was not good at.

"Roz, look at me." She did, her eyes barely discernible in the dark as he fumbled his way through. "Don't let your father's pigheadedness color your opinion of yourself. No one here is judging you for your sins. The reason I got testy is solely because I'm a jerk who doesn't like to share. My mom has been mine alone for a long time. We're a unit. I didn't want to lose that, or have that diluted somehow if you… Wow, this sounds really bad out loud."

She smiled with the faintest stirrings of tenderness. "No, it sounds honest. Which I like."

"This is me being honest," he agreed. If that was all she was looking for, maybe he didn't have to botch this too badly. "So you have to believe me when I say earlier was a combination of you in that dress and me being territorial. And maybe a bit of foot-in-mouth disease."

Her laugh washed through him, dissolving a lot of the tension, and he had to fight the muscles in his hand so that he didn't reach for her. The reasons he wanted to were totally mixed up and he didn't fully understand this urge to connect himself with that laugh in a way that had nothing to do with sex.

"Honesty is the best policy. So I'll return the favor. I don't remember my mom from when she was healthy. I just remember her sick and in a hospital bed, dying. Today a woman I admire invited me to lunch for the first time in my adult life. The fact that she's your mother didn't even factor into why it meant so much to me. Are you starting to see why I got a little bent out of shape about you getting bent out of shape?"

Her tone walloped him, dredging through his gut with razor-sharp teeth. He'd behaved like a jackass and stabbed at Roz's wounds at the same time. This wasn't a run-of-the-mill fight, like what normal couples might go through. They were surfacing enormously difficult emotions that he shouldn't want any part of.

But he was still here.

"If I say I'm sorry, will that help?"

Her smile widened. "Maybe."

Hell, why was he fighting this insanely strong urge to touch her? He skimmed his fingertips down her jaw and feathered a thumb across her lips. "I'm sorry."

She didn't even blink, just leaned until her lips hit his, and then treated him to the longest, sweetest kiss of his experience. Everything fell away except her and he froze, letting her drive this to whatever completion she wished because this was about feeling her out, learning who she was besides the woman he'd had hot, dirty sex with in Vegas.

God, he'd needed this, needed her in ways he wouldn't have guessed. The anticipation of getting her into his arms just like this flavored it so heavily that kissing her was nearly mind-altering. And this wasn't even close to the kind of kiss he'd envisioned jumping into all night. This was something else.

She pulled back and tilted her forehead to his until they touched. "I'm sorry, too. For being difficult. But not for kissing you. You needed the reminder that *we're* a unit. Peanut butter and jelly."

Yes. *That's* what it was. A solidifying of their union. No longer was this a marriage favor he was doing for his mother. He and Roz were becoming something. What, he wasn't sure yet, but it was so much more real than what he'd envisioned.

No. That wasn't what was happening here. Something lodged in his chest and he couldn't breathe all at once. He *couldn't* care about Roz, not like they were a couple. Not like there was any possibility of something deeper than a surface connection that started and ended with sex.

She didn't think there was something bigger than a marriage of convenience happening here. Did she? Had he messed up her expectations with all the talk of dates and getting to know each other? Had he screwed up his *own* expectations?

Surely not. Maybe some things had gotten a little out of whack, strictly due to the rules she'd laid down. The solution was to marry her and get to the place where he could block all that out with lots of hot sex, obviously. The lack of it was throwing them both off, that was all. He'd been forced into this pseudo-intimacy because of the scandal and now that he'd proven he wasn't a sex addict, it was time to move on to the next level. Once things were on familiar ground, he could fix all their fights with orgasms and then no one had to apologize for anything.

"We've got to get a wedding date on the calendar and you in a dress," he muttered.

The sooner the better.

Six

Somehow, Hendrix pulled off a miracle and got the wedding planned in record time, even down to the last place-setting. Roz wasn't confused about his motivation. She'd thrown down a gauntlet that they couldn't have sex until the wedding and had unwittingly created an environment that meant they'd be tense and irritable around each other.

Frankly, she was a little tired of it, too. They didn't have anything in common other than blind lust and a desire to fix the scandal. She got that. Their one disastrous attempt at a date had ended with solid reminders that her skill set didn't extend to forming connections with people, especially not with men—because she was good at having sex with them, but nothing else. Hendrix was no exception.

After her patient attempt to work through his unexpected freak-out over what should have been a simple announcement that she'd had lunch with Helene, his response? *Let's get you in a wedding dress so I can finally get what I came for.*

Fine. They weren't a real unit. Not like Hendrix and Helene, and the reminder had been brutal. Maybe she'd started to feel a little mushy about the idea of being part of something, but it had been nothing but a mirage.

They were getting married for reasons that had nothing to do with peanut butter and jelly and she'd agreed to that. It was smart. Not romantic, and that was a good thing. Less painful in the long run.

She liked orgasms as much as the next girl, so there was really no downside. Except for the niggling feeling that she and Hendrix had been on the verge of something special in the car and then it had vanished.

Her life was spiraling out of her control faster than she could grab on to it. She combated that by sticking her fingers in her ears and pretending there was no wedding planning going on. Hendrix handled it all, finally getting the message after his fourth attempt to include her in the decisions. Except for the flowers she'd already picked out, she really didn't care.

None of it mattered. They'd be undoing it all in a matter of months. The wedding music would dwindle from everyone's memory the moment the last note faded. Who cared what the piece was called?

The morning of the wedding dawned clear and beautiful, a rare day in Raleigh when the humidity wasn't oppressive. Figured. It was a perfect scenario to wear her hair down, but the pearl-encrusted bodice of her dress required her hair to be up. She dragged herself out of bed and got started on enjoying her wedding day—likely the only one she'd ever get. If nothing else, by the end of it, she and Hendrix would be past the weirdness that had sprung up since their date.

Lora picked her up at nine to take her to the spa, where they'd planned to spend the morning pampering themselves, but Roz couldn't get into the spirit. Hell, what kind of spirit was she supposed to be in on the day of a wedding that was basically an arranged marriage? She'd moved a few things into Hendrix's mansion in Oakwood yesterday and they planned to live together for a few months, at least until the election, at which point they'd agreed to reevaluate. Everything was on track.

The spa did not relax her. The masseur had ham hands, the girl who did Roz's bikini wax burned herself—not badly, but she'd had to find someone else to finish the job—and the facial left Roz's skin feeling raw and slightly dry, so her makeup wouldn't apply correctly. Gah, she'd been putting on foundation for fifteen-plus years. Why did her face suddenly look like the Grand Canyon in miniature?

Nerves. So much was riding on this marriage. Her reputation. Clown-Around. Helene's campaign. Her father's political ambitions. And maybe deep inside, she hoped that saying *I do* would magically shift things between her and her father. It wasn't a crime to hope.

But neither was any shifting likely. So far, he'd stayed on script, expressing nonverbal disapproval in the usual ways while tossing out backhanded comments about getting chummy with Helene. It had soured her lunch dates with Hendrix's mom to the point where she had canceled the last one. It had killed her to lose that one-on-one time with Helene but Hendrix had been so weird about it that Roz figured it was better not to get too attached. Her response was mostly self-preservation at this point.

As she leaned into the mirror to work on her eyeliner, her hand started to shake.

Lora glanced over from her spot next to the bride. "You okay? You've been jumpy since this morning."

Dang it. If Lora had noticed, Hendrix would, too. Maybe she could sneak a glass of white wine from the reception before walking down the aisle. Just to settle things inside. "Brides are allowed to be jumpy."

Her friend eyed her. "But this isn't a real wedding. You've been so calm and collected this whole time. It's kind of a shock to see you having this strong of a reaction."

"It is a real wedding," she corrected, fielding a little shock of her own that Lora had classified it any other way. "And a real marriage. I'm taking his name. We'll be sleeping in the same bed. Can't get much more real than that."

That started tonight. Holy hell. That was a lot of reality, orgasms notwithstanding. She'd be an honest-to-God wife who could legally sign her name Mrs. Harris. It suddenly felt like a huge gamble with no guarantee of a payoff.

Lora shrugged and tossed her long blond hair over her shoulder, leaning into the mirror to apply her own cosmetics. "But you're not in love. It's not like he swept you off your feet with a romantic proposal that you couldn't resist. I'm kind of surprised you're going through with it, actually. You didn't plan one tiny part of the ceremony. I had to force you to pick a dress."

All of that was true. And sad all at once that such a cold recitation of facts so accurately described her wedding day. She tossed her head. "I never dreamed of my wedding or scrawled my future married name on stray pieces of paper growing up. I'm marrying a man with bedroom skills a gigolo would envy. My life will not suck. And when we get tired of each other, I get a no-fault divorce. It's a business arrangement. It's the perfect marriage for me."

She'd keep telling herself that until *she* believed it too, and ignore the huge gap in her chest that she wished was filled with something special.

Grinning, Lora waved her mascara wand in Roz's direction. "When you put it that way… Does he have a friend?"

"Sure. I'll introduce you to Warren. You'll like him." Doubtful. Lora wouldn't look twice at a man who accessorized with his cell phone 24/7. "Hendrix's other friend is married."

Jonas and Viv had come across as one of those couples who were really in love. You could just tell they both firmly believed they'd found their soul mate. Honestly, Roz thought she'd be exactly like that if she ever fell in love, which was why she hoped she never did. Her parents had been mad for each other and watching her father waste away alongside her dying mother had been a huge wake-up call. Love equaled pain. And then when it was gone, she envisioned being alone for the rest of her life, just like her father. Carpenters weren't good at serial marriage.

The one she'd get with Hendrix Harris *was* perfect for her.

Hendrix sent a limo to pick up the bride and bridesmaid. Roz felt a little silly at the size of the vehicle when she spread out her white pearl-encrusted skirt on the spacious leather seat that could have held four people. But the fact of the matter was that she didn't have a lot of friends that she would have asked to be in her wedding party. She had acquaintances. They'd all been invited to the social event of the season, though she didn't fool herself for a moment that they were coming for any other reason than morbid curiosity.

All at once, the door to the chapel loomed and her feet carried her into the church's vestibule without much conscious effort on her part. Her father waited for her inside as arranged, but she couldn't quite shake the feeling of walking through a surreal dream.

"Roz," her father called as he caught sight of her. "You're looking well."

Geez. Exactly what every bride dreams of hearing on her wedding day. "Thanks, Dad."

He wasn't effusive with his praise, never had been. But was it too much to ask for a little affection on a day when she was doing something that would benefit him?

Crooking his elbow in her direction, he stood where the coordinator directed him to and then it was Roz's turn to get in line behind Lora, who was stunning in a pale pink column dress with a long skirt. It would have been more appropriate for an evening wedding, but that was one thing Roz had cared about picking out. She'd gotten the dress that looked good on Lora, not the one societal convention dictated.

She was still Rosalind Carpenter. For about thirty more minutes. Oh, God.

What if this was a huge mistake?

Music swelled from the interior of the chapel that Hendrix had insisted would lend validity to their union. That seemed be the litmus test for pretty much all of his wedding decisions—how legit the thing was. She'd never have pegged him as that much of a traditionalist but she got more than an eyeful of his idea of what a proper wedding looked like as the coordinator flung open the doors to the chapel, signaling their entrance.

Five hundred guests rose dutifully to their feet, heads craned toward Roz for their first glimpse of the bride. An explosion of color greeted her, from the bouquets at the end of each pew to the multiple stands holding baskets of blooms across the front. Hendrix had chosen pinks to complement Lora's dress, but hadn't seemed too inclined to stick with a flower theme. There were stargazer lilies she'd picked out at the florist, but also roses, baby's breath, tulips, daisies, and something that might be a larkspur, but her father started down the aisle before she could verify.

Wow, was it hot in here. Every eye in the house was trained on her. Her spine stiffened and she let her own vision blur so she didn't have to see whether they were quietly judging her or had a measure of compassion reflected on their faces. No way was it the latter. No one in attendance had a clue how difficult today was for the motherless bride.

Then her gaze drifted past all the flowers and landed on the star of the show. Hendrix. She stared into his pale hazel eyes as her father handed her off in the most traditional of exchanges. Her husband-to-be clasped her fingers and the five hundred people behind her vanished as she let Hendrix soak through her to the marrow.

"You're so beautiful it hurts inside when I look at you," he murmured.

Her knees turned to marshmallow and she tightened her grip on his hand.

That was the proper thing to say to a bride on her wedding day and she didn't even try to squelch the bloom of gratitude that had just unfurled in her chest. "I bet you say that to all your brides."

He grinned and faced the minister, guiding her through the ceremony like a pro when nerves erased her memory of the rehearsal from the night before. The space-time continuum bent double on itself and the ceremony wound to a close before she'd barely blinked once.

"You may kiss the bride," the minister intoned and that's when she realized the complete tactical error she'd made.

She had to kiss Hendrix. For real. And the moratorium on that thus far had guaranteed this would become A Moment. The carnal spike through the gut at the thought did not bode well for how the actual experience would go down.

Neither did the answering heat in his expression. He cupped her jaw on both sides, giving her plenty of time to think about it. No need. Her whole body had just incinerated with the mere suggestion of the imminent follow-through.

And then he leaned in to capture her mouth with his. It was a full-on assault to the senses as their lips connected and she couldn't do anything else but fling her arms around his waist, or she'd have ended up on the ground, a charred shell that was burned beyond recognition.

Oh God, yes. With that one hard press of his mouth, Hendrix consumed her. This kiss was but a shadow of the many, many others they'd shared, but it was enough to slide memories along her skin, through her core.

This was so very right, so perfect between them. Everything else faded—the weirdness, the nerves. This heat she understood, craved. If he was burning her alive from the inside out, she didn't have to think about all the reasons this marriage might not work.

He teased the flame in her belly into a full raging fire with little licks of his tongue against hers. Hell, that blaze hadn't ever really been extinguished from the moment he'd lit that match in Vegas. Masterfully, the man kissed her until she'd been scraped raw, panting for more, nearly weeping with want.

This was why she'd thrown down the no-kissing-no-sex rule. She could not resist him, even in a church full of people. Her body went into some kind of Hendrix-induced altered state where nothing but basic need existed. And he wasn't even in full-on seduction mode. Thank God he'd played by her rules or there was no telling what new and more horrific scandals might have cropped up prior to the wedding.

That was enough to get her brain back in gear. She broke off the kiss to the sound of flutes and strings. The recessional music. They were supposed to walk and smile now. Somehow, that's what happened and then she floated through a million photographs, a limo ride to the reception and about a million well-wishers.

All she really wanted was to dive back into Hendrix and never surface.

The crowd at the reception crushed that hope flat. No less than ten people vied for their attention at any given time and she'd lost count of the number of times Hendrix had introduced her to someone from his business world. The reverse wasn't at all true, a sobering fact that brought home the reasons she was wearing a wedding band.

She'd spent the past few years having what she'd

staunchly defend as a "good time" but in reality was a panacea for the pain of losing first her mother to cancer and then her father to indifference and grief. The scandals were just the cherry on top of her messy life and ironically, also the reason she couldn't move forward with something respectable like running a charity.

Her new husband would change all of that. Had already started to.

The pièce de résistance of the event came with the first dance between husband and wife. Hendrix, whom she'd scarcely said two words to since that pantie-melting kiss, whisked her out onto the dance floor. He drew her close and when his arms came around her, the strangest sensation floated through her as they began to move to the classical piece that she'd have never picked out but fitted the occasion.

"Hey," he murmured into her ear. "How is Mrs. Harris doing?"

"I don't know. I haven't spoken to your mother." When he laughed, she realized he hadn't meant Helene. "Ha, ha. I'm out of sorts. It's been a long day."

"I know. That's why I asked. You seem distracted."

She pulled back a touch to look at him. "Ask me again."

The smile in his eyes warmed her, but then it slid away to be replaced by something else as their gazes held in a long moment that built on itself with heavy implications. "How are you, Mrs. Harris?"

A name shouldn't have so much color to it. If anything, it should have sounded foreign to her, but it wasn't strange. It felt…good. She took a deep breath and let that reality expand inside her. *Mrs. Harris.* That was her name. Rosalind Harris. Mrs. Roz Harris.

She liked it. Maybe she *should* have practiced writing it out a bajillion times on a piece of scratch paper. Then the concept wouldn't have been such a shock. There was a huge difference between academically knowing that you were changing your name and actually hearing someone address you that way. Especially when the man doing the addressing had the same name and you were married to him.

"I'm better now," she told him.

Understatement. Hendrix was solid and beautiful and he'd pulled off the wedding event of the season. Why hadn't she participated more in the planning?

Sour grapes. Nothing more complicated than that. She'd started getting a little too touchy-feely with the peanut butter and jelly analogy and he'd set her back on the right path with timely reminders of what they were doing here. For his trouble, she'd frozen him out and then used that as an excuse to pull back from a friendship with his mother.

Well, she was over it. They were married now

and both of them knew the score. The no-sex rule wasn't in the way any longer. Thank God. They could spend all their time in bed and never have to talk about mothers, peanut butter or anything difficult.

"This was amazing," she said earnestly. "So much more than I was expecting. Thank you."

Surprise filtered through his expression. "I… You're welcome. I'm glad you liked it. The wedding planner did all the work. I just approved everything."

"I should have done it with you." The fact that she hadn't made her feel petty and childish. If nothing else, it was an effort that benefited her, so she could have done half the work. Then maybe she'd feel more like she'd earned the right to be called Mrs. Harris. "I'm sorry I didn't."

For the first time since their disastrous date, Hendrix smiled at her like he had that night in Vegas. As if he'd found the end of the rainbow and the pot of gold there was more valuable than he'd ever dreamed.

She liked it when he looked at her like that.

"It's okay. It wasn't any trouble." He spun her around as the last notes of the waltz ended and something a little darker and more sensual wafted from the string quartet on the dais in the corner. His arms tightened, drawing her deeper into his embrace. The crowd on the dance floor grew thicker as people filled in around them. "I'm enjoying the benefits of it, so it's all good."

His body pressed against hers deliciously. A slow simmer flared up in her core, bubbling outward until her nerve endings were stretched taut with anticipation. "The benefits?"

"Dancing with my bride, for one," he murmured. His hands drifted along her body with sensual intent, pressing her more firmly against him as he stroked her waist, the curve of her hip, lower still, and there was so much wedding dress in the way that she strained against his touch, yearning for the heat of his hand in places that hadn't been *touched* in so very long.

Dancing was a great excuse to let Hendrix put his hands on her in public. "I'm enjoying that part, too."

"It's been a long time," he said gruffly, "since I had free rein to hold you like this."

Yes, and judging by the oh-so-nice hard length buried in her stomach, he was as affected by their close proximity as she was. "You were a trouper about it."

"Wasn't easy. But it's over now. I can kiss you whenever I feel like it." To prove the point, he nuzzled her neck, setting off fireworks beneath her skin as he nibbled at the flesh.

"That's not kissing," she muttered, biting back a gasp as he cruised to her ear, molding it to his lips as he laved at her lobe.

"I'm getting there."

"Get there faster."

He pulled back and swept her with a glance that was equal parts evaluation and equal parts *I'm a second from throwing you down right here, right now.* "Is that your way of saying you're ready to leave?"

"We can't," she reminded him and tried to ignore how desperately disappointed she sounded.

This was a networking event as much as it was a wedding. Helene had a throng of people around her, and the movers and shakers of Raleigh stood at the bar. If the bride and groom dashed for the door fifteen minutes after the reception started, that wouldn't go over well.

"No," he agreed and bit out a vile curse that perfectly mirrored her thoughts. "We need tongues wagging with positive comments about us, preferably with lots of praise about how respectable we are."

Exactly. Especially if they spouted off at the mouth around her father. He needed a whole lot of reassurance that Roz had turned a corner, that her photo ops with naked men were a thing of the past. From here on out, the only scandal associated with her name should be more along the lines of serving the wrong wine at a party she and Hendrix threw for Harris Tobacco Lounge executive staff.

"So maybe we don't leave," she said as a plausible alternative began to form in her mind. Oh God, did she need that alternative. Fast. Her insides were already tight and slick with need.

His expression turned crafty as he considered her comment. "Maybe not. Maybe there's a…closet in the back?"

"With a door. That locks."

His thumb strayed to the place along her bodice where it met the skin of her back and heat flashed as he caressed the seam, dipping inside just enough to drive her insane and then skimming along until he hit the zipper.

"One tug, and this would be history," he said, the hazel in his eyes mesmerizing her with the promise as he toyed with the hook anchoring the zipper to the bodice. "It feels complicated. Challenging."

"Maybe you don't start there," she suggested and swayed a little to give the couples around them the impression the bride and groom were still dancing when in reality, her attention was on the perimeter of the room where two very promising hallways led to the back of the reception venue. "You might have better luck checking out how easily my skirt lifts up."

"Mrs. Harris, I do like the way you think." In a flash, he grabbed her hand and spun to lead her from the dance floor.

Well then. Looked like the honeymoon was starting early. She had no problem with that and she was nothing if not ready to ignore the fact that the bride and groom were still dashing for the door fifteen minutes after the reception started but with this plan, they'd be back in a few minutes. At least ten. Maybe once wouldn't be enough. Was married sex better than one night stand sex? Oh God, she couldn't wait to find out.

Breathlessly, she followed him, ignoring the multitudes of people who called out to them as they scouted for this hypothetical closet with a door that locked. In a true wedding day miracle, off the kitchen there was a linen closet full of spare tablecloths and empty centerpieces. No one saw them duck through the door, or at least no one who counted. They passed a member of the waitstaff who pretended he hadn't noticed their beeline through the back rooms where guests typically didn't tread. Whether it was a testament to his discretion or the fact that Hendrix and Roz were tied to powerful families, she didn't know. Didn't care.

All that mattered was the door had a lock. She shut it behind her with a click and flipped the dead bolt, plunging the room into semidarkness. Maybe there was a light but before she could reach for it, Hendrix pinned her against the door, his mouth on hers in an urgent, no-holds-barred kiss. No time to search for a light. No time to care.

Her knees gave out as the onslaught liquefied her entire body, but he'd wedged one leg so expertly between hers that she didn't melt to the ground in a big hot puddle. She moaned as his tongue invaded her mouth, heated and insistent against hers. He hefted her deeper into his body as he shifted closer.

Too many clothes. She got to work on his buttons, cursing at the intricacy of his tuxedo. Shame she couldn't just rip the little discs from the fabric but they had to reappear in public. Soon. Giving up, she pulled the fabric from his waistband so she could slide her hands under it.

Oh, yes, he was warm and his body was still drool-worthy with ridges and valleys of muscle along his abs that her fingers remembered well. He pressed closer still, trapping her hands between them, which was not going to work, so she shifted to the back as he gathered up her skirts, bunching the fabric at her waist. Instantly, she regretted not making him take the time to pull the dress off. She wanted his hands everywhere on her body, but then she forgot to care because his fingers slid beneath the white lacy thong she'd donned this morning in deference to her wedding day.

"I want to see this thong later," he rumbled in her ear as he fingered the panties instead of the place she needed him most. "It feels sexy and tiny and so good."

"It feels in the way," she corrected and gasped as he yanked the panties off, letting them fall to her ankles. She toed off the fabric and kicked it aside. She needed him back in place *now.* "Touch me. Hurry."

Fast. Hard. Frenzied. These were the things she wanted, not a speech about her undergarments. This was sex in its rawest form and she knew already that it would be good between them. She hoped it would put them on familiar ground. Eliminate confusion about what they were doing here.

"What's your rush, Mrs. Harris?" He teased her with short little caresses of his fingertips across her shoulder, down her cleavage, which ached for his attention, but had far too many seed pearls in the way for that nonsense.

"Besides the hundreds of people waiting for us?" Her back arched involuntarily as his fingers found their way beneath the tight bodice of her dress to toy with her breasts. Heavenly heat corkscrewed through her core as he fingered her taut, sensitized nipples.

"Besides that."

"You're my rush," she ground out. "I'm about to come apart and I need your hands on me."

She needed oblivion like only he could give her, where all she could do was feel. Then it didn't matter that he was totally on board with a closet quickie for their first time together as husband and wife. Neither of them did intimacy. It was what made their marriage so perfect.

"Like this?" His hand snaked between them to

palm her stomach and she wiggled, hoping to get it lower. He complied inch by maddening inch, creeping toward the finish line with a restraint more suited for a choirboy than the bad boy she knew lurked in his heart.

He'd licked her in places that had never been touched by a man. He'd talked so dirty while doing it that she could practically give herself an orgasm thinking about it. They were having sex in a closet with five hundred oblivious people on the other side of the wall and he had every bit of the skill set necessary to make it intoxicating. She needed *that* man.

"Hendrix, please," she begged. "I'm dying here."

"I've been dying for weeks and weeks," he said and she groaned as he wandered around to the back, wedging his hand between her buttocks and the door to play with flesh that certainly appreciated his attention but wasn't the part that needed him most.

Practically panting, she circled her hips, hoping he'd get the hint that the place he should be focusing on was between her thighs. "So this is my punishment for not letting you have your way with me until now?"

"Oh, no, sweetheart. This is my reward," he murmured. "I've dreamed of having you in my arms again so I could feel your amazing body in a hundred different ways. Like this."

Finally, he let his fingers walk through her center, parting the folds to make way, and one slid deep inside. Mewling because that was the only sound she could make, she widened herself for him, desperate for more instantly, and he obliged with another finger, plunging both into her slickness with his own groan.

"I could stay here for an eternity," he whispered. "But I need to—"

He cursed as she eased her way into his pants, too blind with need to bother with the zipper. Oh, yes, there he was. She palmed his hot, hard length through his underwear and it wasn't enough. "I need, too."

Urgently, she fumbled with his clothes and managed to get the buttons of his shirt partially undone, hissing as he withdrew his magic hands from her body to help. But that was a much better plan because his progress far eclipsed hers and he even had the wherewithal to find a condom from somewhere that she distinctly heard him tear open. That was some amazing foresight that she appreciated.

Then her brain ceased to function as he boosted her up against the door with one arm, notched his hard tip at her entrance and pushed. Stars wheeled across her vision as he filled her with his entire glorious length. Greedily, she took him, desperate for more, desperate for all of it, and he gave it to her, letting her slide down until they were nested so deep that she could feel him in her soul.

No.

No, she could not. That was far too fanciful for what was happening here. This was sex. Only. Her body craved friction, heat, a man's hard thrusts. Not poetry.

Wrapping her legs around him, she gripped his shoulders, letting her fingers sink into the fabric covering them because even if it left marks, who cared? They were married and no one else would see his bare shoulders but her.

He growled his approval and it rumbled through her rib cage. Or maybe that was the avalanche of satisfaction cascading through her chest because Hendrix was hers. No other woman got to see him naked. It shouldn't feel so good, so significant. But there was no escaping the fact that they were a unit now whether he liked it or not.

They shared a name. A house. Mutual goals. If he didn't like peanut butter and jelly, he should have come up with another plan to fix the scandal.

Shifting ever so slightly, he hit a spot inside her that felt so good it tore tears from her eyes. The position sensitized her to the point of madness and she urged him on with her hips as he drove them both into the stratosphere, the door biting into her back as she muffled her cries against his suit jacket, praying she wasn't smearing makeup all over his shoulder.

That would be a dead giveaway to anyone who bothered to notice. And she liked the idea of keeping this encounter secret. Their own little wedding party.

Explosion imminent, she rolled her hips until the angle increased the pressure the way she liked it. Hendrix grabbed one thigh, opening her even wider, and that was it. The orgasm ripped through her and she melted against him, going boneless in his arms until his own cry signaled his release.

He gave them both about five seconds of recovery time and then let her legs drift to the floor so they could hold each other up. Which she gladly did because he'd earned it.

"That was great for starters," she muttered against his shoulder because it felt expected that she should reiterate how hot—and not meaningful—this encounter was. "I can definitely report that took the edge off, but I'm nowhere near done."

There was so much more to explore. Best part? She could. Whenever she felt like it, since they'd be sleeping in the same bed. Married sex had a lot to recommend it.

Someone rattled the doorknob, nearly startling out of her skin.

"You have the key?" a muffled voice from the other side of the wall called.

Oh, God. They were about to be discovered.

Seven

Where was her underwear? It was so dark in here. Had she kicked them to the left? Panic drained Roz's mind and she couldn't think.

The doorknob rattled again. Whoever it was probably had no idea that the bride and groom were in the closet. But they were probably packing a cell phone with a camera. They always were.

Stuffing her fist against her mouth, Roz jumped away from the door and knelt to feel around for her panties, dress impeding her progress like a big white straitjacket for legs. Hendrix fumbled with his own clothes. His zipper shushed, sounding like an explosion in the small room. At least he'd gotten that much covered. Any photographs of this tryst would be of the dressed variety. But still not the commemorative moment they'd like captured digitally for eternity.

The door swung open, spilling light into the closet, and Roz had a very nasty flashback to a similar moment when she was twenty, with the obvious difference this time being that she was wearing a wedding dress and the man tucking in his shirt behind her had recently signed a marriage license.

Two white-coated waiters stared at her and Hendrix and she'd like to say her years of practice at being caught in less-than-stellar circumstances had prepared her for it, but it was never as easy as tossing her hair back and letting the chips fall where they may.

Besides, she refused to be embarrassed. Everything was covered. Married people were allowed to be in a locked closet without fear of judgment—or she wouldn't have bothered to go through with all of this. The wait staff was interrupting *her*, not the other way around.

She shot to her feet and it was a testament to her feigned righteous indignation at being disturbed that she didn't break an ankle as one of her stilettos hit the ground at an awkward angle.

"Um, sorry," the one on the left said, and he might as well have hashtagged it *#notsorry*.

His face beamed his prurient delight, like something naughty was showing, and she had half a moment of pure horror over not actually locating her underwear. She tugged on her skirt to make sure it wasn't caught on itself, but then Hendrix came up behind her, snaking an arm around her waist. Claiming her. They were a unit and he had her back.

She leaned into him, more grateful than she had a right to be.

"Can you give us a minute?" he said smoothly to the interrupters and actually waited for the one waiter's nod before he shut the door in their face. Brilliant. Why hadn't she thought of that?

Hendrix flipped on the overhead light, the white lace scrap on the floor easily identifiable at that point. But instead of letting her fetch her panties, he tipped her chin up and laid a kiss on her lips that had nothing to do with sex. Couldn't. There were people outside who wanted inside this closet and they'd been busted.

"I wasn't finished, either," he murmured against her mouth by way of explanation.

She nodded, letting his warmth bleed through her via their joined lips, mystified why that sweet, unnecessary cap to their closet hookup meant so much. Eventually, he let her go and they got everything situated well enough to mix in polite company again. Hendrix reopened the door and they slipped past the waiters hand in hand.

Her husband's palm burned against hers. She couldn't recall the last time someone had held her hand, like they were boyfriend-girlfriend. Or whatever. They were married. Nothing wrong with holding hands. It was just…unexpected.

"You okay?" Hendrix said softly, pulling her to the side of the short hallway that led to the reception area. His attention was firmly on her, but before she could answer or figure out why his concern had just squished at a place inside, more people interrupted them.

Why couldn't everyone leave them alone so she could spend about a dozen hours exploring why everything with Hendrix felt so different now that she'd signed a piece of paper?

Hendrix's arm went tense under her fingers and she turned. Her father. And Helene. They stood at the end of the short hall, varying expressions of dismay and relief spreading across their faces.

Oh, God. The very people they were trying to help with this scandal-fixing marriage. Now it was obvious to everyone that she couldn't resist Hendrix, that she had something wrong with her that made it impossible to wait for more appropriate circumstances before getting naked with the man.

"We got a little concerned when we couldn't find you," Helene said with a smile. "But here you are."

Her father didn't smile. He crossed his arms and even though he could look her in the eye when she wore stilettos, she still felt small and admonished even before he opened his mouth. Marrying Hendrix had been a last-ditch effort to do *something* her father approved of. Looked like that had been a vain effort all the way around.

"Glad to see that you're dressed," her father said and it was clear that he was speaking directly to his daughter.

The *for once* was implied and sure enough, flooded her with the embarrassment she'd managed to fight off earlier, after being discovered by wait staff. Thank God their parents hadn't been the ones to fling open that door.

"That's not really your concern any longer," Hendrix said to her father.

She did a double take. Was he sticking up for her?

"It is my concern," her father corrected. "This marriage isn't guaranteed to remove all of the social shame from the photographs. Additional fodder could still be harmful and Roz is quite good at feeding that fire."

"Still not your concern," Hendrix corrected mildly and his hand tightened around hers.

As a warning to let him handle it? She couldn't speak anyway. The knot in her throat had grown big enough to choke a hippopotamus.

"Roz is my wife," Hendrix continued. "And any bad press that comes her way is my responsibility to mitigate. She has my name now. I'll take care of her."

Okay, there might be crying in her immediate future.

"Hendrix," she murmured because she felt like she had to say something, but that was as much as her brain could manufacture.

With that, her husband nodded to his mother and swept Roz past the inquisition that should have ruined her day. Instead, Hendrix had relegated that confrontation to an insignificant incident in the hall.

How had he done that? She snuck a glance at him. "Thank you. You didn't have to do that."

He shot her an enigmatic smile. "I did so have to do that. Your father should be proud of you, not throwing you to the wolves."

"Um, yeah. He's never really appreciated my ability to keep my balance while having sex against a door."

Hendrix laughed at that, which actually made her relax for what felt like the first time all day.

"I appreciate that skill." He waggled his brows and guided her back into the reception where they were swallowed by the crowd, none of whom seemed to notice they'd been gone.

If it was at all possible to receive an indicator that she'd made the right decision in marrying Hendrix Harris, that moment with her father had been it. Half of her reason for agreeing had to do with gaining approval from a man who had demonstrated time and time again that she could not earn his respect no matter what. That possibility had been completely eliminated…only to be replaced with a completely different reality.

Her husband wasn't going to take any crap from her father.

Maybe she didn't have to, either.

And that's when she actually started enjoying her wedding day.

Despite Paul Carpenter's comments to the contrary, the wedding had apparently gone a long way toward smoothing over the scandal. The snide looks Hendrix had witnessed people shooting at Roz when they'd gone to the florist, and even to some degree during their one date, had dwindled. There were lots of smiles, lots of congrats, lots of schmoozers.

And what kind of crap was that?

It was one thing to have an academic understanding that they were getting married so that Helene Harris for Governor didn't take unnecessary hits, but it was another entirely to see it in action. Especially when he was starting to suspect that some of the issue had to do with what society perceived as his "bad taste" to have mixed it up with the wild Carpenter daughter.

He was fixing it for her. Not the other way around. What was just as crazy? He liked being her go-to guy. The dressing-down he'd given her father had felt good. No one deserved to be judged for a healthy sexual appetite when her partner was a consenting adult.

He needed to get the hell out of here and make some wedding day memories at home, where his wife could do whatever she so desired without anyone knowing about it.

"Let's go," he growled in Roz's ear. "We've been social for like a million hours already. Everyone here can suck it."

"Including me?" Her gaze grew a hungry edge that had all kinds of appealing implications inside it, especially when she dragged it down his body. "Because coincidentally, that's exactly what I had in mind."

"Really?" His groin tightened so fast it made him light-headed.

"True story," she murmured. "Or didn't you get the memo earlier that I wasn't done?"

Wheeling, he waved at his mother and snagged Roz's hand to lead her to the limo that waited patiently for them at the curb of the North Ridge Country Club. He'd paid the wedding coordinator a hefty sum to manage the logistics of the reception; she could handle whatever came after the departure of the bride and groom.

The limo ride took far too long—a whole ten minutes, during which he kept his hands off Roz like a good boy because this time, he didn't want quick.

Slow would be the theme of his wedding night.

Except his wife smelled divine and she cuddled up next to him on the roomy leather seat, letting her fingers do some serious wandering over his lap. Strands of Roz's dark hair had pulled out of the bun-like thing at her crown, dripping down in sexy little tendrils, and all he could think about was how it had gotten that way—his fingers.

He'd like to tug on a few more strands while deep inside her.

By the time the limo pulled up to the house, which his housekeeper had lit up for their arrival, his hard-on could cut glass and his patience had started to unravel.

"Inside," he growled. "Now."

To help her along, he swept her up in his arms to carry her over the threshold because it seemed like a legit thing that people did on their wedding day. She snuggled down into his embrace, looping her arms around his neck, and then got busy testing out his ability to walk while she nibbled on the flesh near his ear. Her tongue flicked out, sending a shower of sparks down his throat, and he stumbled, catching himself immediately. Wouldn't do to drop his new wife.

"Unless you'd like our wedding night to be memorialized with a trip to the ER, I'd suggest waiting five seconds for any more of that," he advised her, which she pretty much ignored. Now that he was on to her and better able to compensate, he walked faster.

They cleared the double front door, barely, as she'd started exploring his collarbone with her lips. There was no way he was doing stairs in his current fully aroused, highly sensitized state, so he let her slide to the ground and hustled her to the second floor.

Roz beat him to the gargantuan master suite that he'd yet to christen properly. He shut the doors to the bedroom behind him. In Vegas, they'd had a strict rule that no surface would go untouched. His bedroom's decor had been pulled together by a professional and contained solid pieces stained with a shade of espresso that was so dark, it looked black. Not one Carpenter piece in the bunch, not even the woman beckoning him with a hooded, enigmatic expression that portrayed her very naughty thoughts.

Good God she was gorgeous in her white dress. She had the fullest lips that needed nothing extra to be lush and inviting. He could write poetry to her mouth for a decade. And her eyes…they did a thing where they were both transparent and mysterious all at the same time.

Would he ever get tired of her face? What if they were the kind of couple who actually stayed married on purpose, affording him the opportunity to watch her age? One day he might wake up and wonder where her looks had gone. But he didn't think so. She'd still be Roz inside and that was the part he wanted with a burning need he scarcely recognized.

And need was supposed to be his wheelhouse. When he couldn't quantify something related to sex, that was a problem. It felt too much like the intimacy that he religiously avoided.

No, the real problem was that they weren't having sex yet. Sex eliminated all of the weirdness with pure mechanics of pleasure. And while he was busy composing sonnets to his wife's beauty, she was standing there staring at him like he'd lost his mind, likely because he hadn't made a move on her yet.

Clearly, he was slightly insane. What was he waiting for?

Striding forward, he did the one thing he hadn't been able to do thus far. He spun his bride to face away from him, undid the catch on her zipper and yanked it down. The strapless dress peeled from her body, baring her back and oh, yeah, that was nice. Her spine beckoned and he bent to fuse his mouth to the ridges, working his way down until he hit the hollow above her buttocks. Laving at it, he adding some lip action until he earned a sharp little gasp from her.

This was what he'd come for. Blinding, carnal pleasure. All of the other internal noise? Not happening. The faster he got to a place where he couldn't think, the faster all of the stuff inside that shouldn't be there would fade.

That spurred him on enough to want more. Easing the dress down her hips, he pushed her gently, encouraging her to step out of it. That sexy little thong that he'd thus far only felt was indeed amazing in the light. It formed a vee down between her cheeks like an arrow pointing the way to paradise and he groaned as he recalled how much time he'd spent pleasuring her in that exact spot while in Vegas. It was worth a repeat for sure.

Falling to his knees, he slid his tongue beneath the lacy bands, following the dip down and back up again. He accompanied that with a leisurely exploration of the backs of her legs, ending with a nice tour of the covered area between her cheeks. That's when her legs started trembling, whether from excitement or exhaustion he couldn't be sure. He'd have to come back later.

Right now, his bride needed to be more comfortable. He had a lot more where that had come from.

He picked her up in his arms again and without the binding dress, it was so much easier. And more rewarding as her bare breasts were *right there* for his viewing pleasure. That was a much better place to focus his attention.

Laying her on the bed, he looked his fill as he stripped out of his own clothes, impressed that he'd found the stamina to take the time. The last sock hit the floor and the appreciation in Roz's gaze as she watched his show thoroughly stirred him.

The closet gymnastics had done nothing to take the edge off. Roz was dead wrong about that. He wanted her all over again with a fierce urgency that demanded absolute surrender.

Crawling across the mattress and up her body, he took the liberty of kissing his way to the perfect globes of her breasts, licking one bright, hard tip into his mouth. Her flesh rolled across his tongue. Divine. He sucked harder and she arched up off the bed with a tiny gasp. Not enough. Teeth against the tip, he scraped at it while plucking at the other one with his fingertips.

She felt exquisite in his hand. Silky. Excited. She pushed against his mouth, shoving her breast deeper, and he took it all, sucking her nipple against the roof of his mouth. That had driven her wild once before.

It did again. That simple movement got her thrashing under him, driving her hips against his painfully hard erection. The contact lit him up and felt so good, he ground into her stomach with tight circles. *Inside. Now.* His body was screaming for release, shooting instructions to his muscles to tilt her hips and drive to completion.

Not on the agenda. Not yet. He had to slow it down. Grabbing her hips, he peeled away from her luscious body and kissed down the length of her stomach until he hit her thighs. That lacy thong covered her and as much as he hated to see it go, it went.

He pushed her legs open and kept going. Gorgeous. The faster he sated her, the slower he could go because she was making him insane with hip rolls that pushed her closer to him, obviously seeking relief from the fire that was licking through her veins.

Or maybe that was just him.

Her secrets spread wide, he paused just a moment to enjoy the visual, but she was having none of that.

"Put your mouth on me," she instructed throatily. "I've dreamed about your wicked hard tongue for weeks and weeks."

Oh yeah? That was enough of a compliment to spur him into action. The first lick exploded across his taste buds, earthy and so thick with her desire. For him. This was his wife, who was wet and slick *for him*. It was nearly spiritual. Why didn't they tell you the mere act of signing a piece of paper had so much significance?

That was a discovery best explored further through hands-on experience. Her juices flowed over his tongue as he drove deeper, added a finger to the party, swirled along her crease until she started bucking against his face and still she seemed to crave more.

He gave it to her, sliding a wet finger between her cheeks to toy with her while simultaneously working the nub at her pleasure center with his teeth. Her thighs clenched, and she rocked against his fingers, pushing them deeper, and then she came with a cry that vibrated through his gut.

That was not something he could possibly hear enough.

She sat up far before he would have said she'd had time to recover, pushed him free of her body and rolled him until she was on top. Looked like they were moving on. Noted. But he couldn't find a thing to complain about as she straddled his hips. She'd never taken off her white strappy stilettos and she parked one on each side of his thighs, easing her center into a place just south of where he really wanted it, but that fit with his need to go slow, so he let her.

He'd teased up a flush along her cheeks and her beautiful peaked nipples rode high on her breasts. As she stared down at him from her perch, she was the most gorgeous thing he'd ever seen, with those pursed lips and a sated sheen in her eyes that he'd been personally responsible for putting there.

He wanted to do it again. And again.

And finally, he could. He reached for her, but she shook her head, clamping her thighs tight against him as she laced his fingers with hers to draw his hands away from her body. She weighed practically nothing and it would be an easy matter to break free, but he was kind of curious what she had in mind that required him to stay still.

He found out when she released his fingers to trail her own down his torso until she reached his groin. All the breath whooshed from his lungs as she palmed him to stroke downward with one hard thrust.

Fire tore through his body in a maelstrom of need.

His eyelids flew shut as he struggled to breathe, to hold it together, to keep from exploding right there in her hand. She wasn't in a merciful mood obviously because she crawled backward to kneel over him, captured his gaze in her hot one, and licked him.

The sight of her pink tongue laving across his flesh nearly undid him. Then she sucked him fully into her mouth and he pulsed against her tongue and it was almost too much to hold back. He clawed back the release with some kind of superpower he had no idea he possessed.

Anti-Orgasm Man. He should get a T-shirt for his effort.

Except his wife had some powers of her own and worked him back into a frenzy in under a minute flat. This was going to be a very short honeymoon indeed if she didn't stop *this instant*.

"Whoa, sweetheart," he bit out hoarsely and

tried to ease out from her mouth without catching his sensitized flesh on her teeth. She pushed him deeper into her throat in response, melting his bones in the process so it was really difficult to get his arms to work.

"Please," he begged as she swirled her tongue counterclockwise so fast that he felt the answering lick of heat explode outward clear to his toes. His head fell backward against the bed as his legs tensed and he genuinely had no clue what he was begging her to do—stop or keep going.

She took the decision out of his hands by purring with him deep in her mouth and the vibration was the tipping point. The release rushed through his veins, gathered at the base of his spine and pushed from his body like a tsunami, eating everything in its path. She took it all and more, massaging him to a brilliant finish that wrung him out. Spent, he collapsed back on the mattress, too drained to move.

"That was for following the rules," she told him with a smug laugh. "You deserve about ten more."

If he'd known that was the prize for proving to himself and everyone else that he could go without sex, it might have made the whole moratorium a lot easier. Without opening his eyes, he nodded. "You have my permission to proceed."

"Ha, I didn't mean right this minute."

She fell silent and the pause was so heavy that he opened his eyes. Roz was lounging on the bed between his thighs, decked out like a naked offering with one leg draped over his calf and an elbow crooked on the far side of his hip. It was the most erotic pose he'd ever seen in his life. And that was saying something considering the sizzle factor of the photograph she'd starred in.

"Thank you," she said. "For what you said to my father."

Her expression was so enigmatic, he couldn't do anything but let his own gaze travel over it in search of clues for what he should say next. *You're welcome* seemed highly lacking in weight given the catch he'd noted in her voice. Neither was this a conversation he wanted to have while in bed with a naked woman.

Except she wasn't any garden-variety naked woman that he had no plans to see again.

It was Roz. And he most definitely would be waking up with her in the morning. So many mornings that he was at a loss how to avoid the significant overtones of this kind of sex, where they were apparently going to talk about stuff between rounds of pleasure.

Maybe that was the key. He just had to move them along until they were back in a place where there was nothing but heat between them. Clearly he hadn't gotten her hot enough yet if she could still think about things outside of this room.

"Let's talk about that later, shall we?" he murmured.

The tendrils of hair around her face had increased exponentially and he itched to pull the entire mass free of its confines. So he indulged himself. Leaning up, he plucked pins from her dark hair. Slowly, he let chunks of hair fall to her shoulders, and the enigmatic, slightly guarded expression melted away.

Better. She deserved about ten more orgasms, too. Enough that she could only focus on how good he could make her feel and not the crappy stuff about her life that he had an inexplicable drive to fix for her.

"Tonight is about making up for lost time," he told her as the last pin fell free. "I thought I'd never see you again after Vegas. I can't lie. I wanted to."

Why had he blurted that out? They were supposed to be reeling back the true confessions, not throwing down more.

She blinked and let the tiniest lift of her lips register. "I'd like to say I forgot about you. I tried. Never happened."

And here they were. Married. It was something he was having difficulty reconciling in his mind when Roz fit so easily into the "hot fling" box in his head. Surely there had been a woman at some point in the past whom he'd seen more than once, but he couldn't recall the face of anyone but this one. She'd filled his thoughts so much over the past month or so that he suddenly feared he'd have a hard time getting her out when they divorced.

More sex needed, stat. Obviously. They were doing far too much chitchatting.

Reaching for her, he snagged her shoulders and hauled her up the length of his body, which went a long way toward reviving him for round two. She met him in a fiery kiss that shot sensation down his throat. Roz spread her legs to straddle him, this time hitting the exact spot he wanted her to be in, apparently on board with no more talking.

The heat built on itself instantly, putting urgency into their kisses, and the thrust of her tongue against his had sweet fire laced through it that he welcomed. This time, there was no need to go slow and he didn't waste the opportunity. Taking a half second to pull out the box of condoms he'd stashed in his bedside table in anticipation of their wedding night, he dove back onto her, rolling to put her under him so he could focus.

She needed oblivion. He could give her that. Taking her mouth in a fierce kiss, he let his hands roam over her amazing body, caressing whatever he could reach until she was moaning deep in her chest. Her blistering fingers closed around his erection, priming it, and then she reached for the condoms before he could. In what might be the hottest thing she'd done thus far, she rolled it on him, squeezing and teasing as she went, then notching him at her entrance.

He caught her gaze as he paused, savoring this moment before he plunged because it was his favorite. The anticipation built and she flexed her hips, eager for him but not taking the initiative, apparently content to let him go at his own pace.

Roz was his match in every way. The reality seeped through him as they stared at each other, their chests heaving with the exertion of holding back. And then he pushed inside and not even the feel of her mouth could match the exquisiteness of the way her silk caressed every millimeter. He sucked in a breath as she took him deeper, wrapping her legs around him to hold him inside.

The pressure and tension climbed until he had to move, to feel. Gasping, she arched against him, grazing her breasts against his torso, and that felt unbelievable, too. Sensation swirled, driving him faster and faster and she closed around him again and again, squeezing until she was crying out her pleasure. His second release built and she was still watching him, her eyes dark and sensual and so open that he fell into them, hopefully never to surface.

They exploded together and it was only as they came down, wrapped in each other's arms, that he realized that they'd done it missionary style, like a real couple. A first. He'd have said he hated that position but it had felt so right with Roz. Something warm lingered in his chest as he pushed hair out of her face. She kissed his temple and snuggled deeper into his embrace.

This was maybe the most sated he'd ever been in his life. And they hadn't even had sex that many times. Quantity had always been his goal in the past, but apparently quality trumped that. Because they'd gotten married? Because he knew they had tomorrow night and the next and the next, so he didn't have to cram all his appetites into a few hours?

Whatever it was, it felt different. He liked it. Who knew?

This was uncharted territory and he didn't quite know what to do with it. Sex hadn't decreased the intimacy quotient after all. But he'd always shied away from that because rejection wasn't something he dealt with well, or rather, more to the point, he'd never felt like finding out how well he'd deal with it.

His father had done such a thorough job of rejecting him that he'd lived most of his life with total hatred of a man he'd never met. That was what had made the pact with Jonas and Warren so easy. He had no interest in learning how much more it would hurt to be rejected by someone he'd fallen in love with. Obviously it had driven Marcus to a permanent solution. What made Hendrix so much more capable of handling the same?

The rational part of his brain kicked in. Honestly, he'd have to give a woman a chance to reject him in order to fully test that.

Had he been given an opportunity to do exactly that? Roz had been great so far in their relationship. Maybe she was the exception to the rule. Maybe he could test out having a little more with her...

He settled her a little closer, letting her warm him thoroughly, and snagged the sheet to cover them. They hadn't slept at all that night in Vegas, so this would be a first, too. Waking up with a woman had also been something he studiously avoided, but waking up with Roz held enormous appeal.

If "more" didn't work out, then they could get a divorce like they'd always planned. It was practically a foolproof experiment in something that he'd never have said he'd want but couldn't seem to stop himself from exploring.

Eight

Hendrix and Roz had opted not to go away for their honeymoon, largely because that was something real couples did. But also because Helene had already scheduled a splashy fundraiser, the biggest one of the summer, for four days after the wedding. The event was supposed to generate the majority of the money needed to push her campaign through to the election. In other words, it was a big deal.

Helene had specifically asked them to make an appearance so it didn't seem like they were hiding. *Go big or go home,* she'd said with a smile and Roz hadn't really been able to find a good argument against attending. Though she'd racked her brain for one because a big social event with plenty of opportunity for her to feel like she still wasn't good enough to be associated with the Harris name didn't sound like fun.

The afternoon of, Hendrix came home from work early carrying a bag emblazoned with the name of an exclusive store that Roz knew only carried women's clothing. Intrigued, she eyed the bag.

"You entering a drag queen revue that I don't know about?" she asked from her perch on the lounger near the window of their bedroom. It was an enormous room in an even more enormous house that felt genuinely empty when her husband wasn't in it. Probably because it was his, not hers.

Or at least that was the excuse she kept telling herself so she didn't have to think about what it meant that she sometimes missed him. That she thought about him all day long and only some of it was sexual.

"Maybe." He waggled his brows. "Let's see if it fits."

He pulled the dress from a layer of tissue paper and held it up to his chest as she giggled over his antics. But then the dress fully unfurled, revealing what he'd picked out. Oh, God, it was gorgeous. Red, with a gold clasp at the waist that gathered the material close.

"I think it would fit me better than you," she said wryly. "Is this your subtle way of getting me excited about the idea of hanging out with North Carolina's movers and shakers?"

"Depends." He shot her an adorable smile that made her pulse beat a little strangely as the dress became the second-most-beautiful thing in the room. "Did it work?"

Oh, it worked all right, but not even close to the way he meant.

"Only if it goes with the gold shoes I have in my closet." She held out a hand for the gown because the whole thing felt inevitable. "I'll try it on. But I'm only wearing it because you picked it out."

The silk slid through her hands like water as she laid it on the couch, then stood to wiggle out of her pants and shirt. The dress was strapless on one side and came up into an elegant over-the-shoulder style on the other. It settled against her curves like it had been made for her and fell to the ground in a waterfall of red. A high slit revealed enough leg to raise some eyebrows, which she sincerely hoped Hendrix would use as a convenient way to get his hands on her during dinner.

"You look amazing," he said quietly and when she glanced at him, pride glinted from his eyes.

"You have good taste," she shot back, mystified why the compliment pleased her so much. The gift as a whole pleased her in ways she'd never have expected. No man had ever bought her clothes before.

She'd never had a need for one to, nor would she have accepted such a gift from anyone else.

Sure, there was an agenda buried in the middle of his gesture. He needed her by his side at his mother's thing and now she couldn't use *I have nothing to wear* as an excuse to weasel out of it. But she didn't care. The dress fit like a dream, clearly indicating her husband paid attention to details, and the way he was looking at her made her feel desired more sharply than anything he'd done in their entire history. That was saying something.

She half expected him to reach for her, but he started chattering about something that had happened at work earlier as he stripped out of his suit, then went to take a shower. Too bad. She'd be happy to show up late but he wasn't on board with that.

The limo ride was uneventful and she started to get antsy. The wedding hadn't been too bad in terms of dirty looks and noses in the air. But she'd been the bride and it was practically a requirement that people treat her nicely on her wedding day. This fundraiser was a whole different ball game and she didn't often do this kind of society thing. For a reason.

Only for Helene would she brave it. And because Hendrix had done something so unexpected as buy her a dress.

"Nervous?" Hendrix murmured as they exited the limo. "I'll hold your hand."

"You're supposed to," she reminded him blithely. "Because we're married and making sure people are fully aware of that fact."

When he clasped her fingers in his, though, it didn't feel utilitarian. Especially when he glanced down at her and smiled like they shared a secret. "I'm also doing it because I want to."

That warmed her enormously. For about two minutes. Because that's when she saw her father. Whom she had not realized would be in attendance. Of course he'd wrangled an invitation to the premiere Helene Harris for Governor event of the season. Maybe Helene had even invited him of her own free will.

Roz's chest turned to ice.

"I wonder if there's a closet in this place," she said into Hendrix's ear with a little nuzzle. If she could entice him into a back hall, they could spend an hour there before anyone even noticed they'd arrived. Then there wouldn't be a big to-do about them disappearing, and she could get good and relaxed before braving the hypercritical looks and comments.

Hendrix smiled at a few people and snaked an arm around Roz, pulling her close. But instead of copping a feel, like she'd have laid odds on, he held her waist in a perfectly respectable fashion. "Maybe we'll look later."

"Maybe we should look now." She slid her own

arm around his waist in kind, but let her hand drift south with a caress designed to remind him they were at their best when they were burning up with need for each other. Though why she had to be the aggressor in this situation, she wasn't quite sure.

Instead of shooting her a salacious grin that communicated all the naughty thoughts in his mind, he pulled her into a shadowy alcove away from the crush. Oh, this had possibilities. The area wasn't enclosed, but could be considered private. Emboldened, she slipped the button free on his tux jacket, gauging exactly how much cover it might provide if he had a mind to get handsy.

That got her a smile, but without much carnal heat laced through it. No worries. She could get him hot and bothered pretty quickly and let her fingers do some walking. But he just laced his fingers with hers and pulled them free of his body.

"Roz, come on."

That didn't sound like the precursor to a hot round of mutual orgasmic delight. "I'm trying to, but you're not helping any."

"Why do we always have to have sex in public?"

Agape, she stared at him. "I must not be doing it right if you have to ask that question."

"I'm being serious." Their fingers were still entwined and he brought one to his mouth to kiss the back of her hand tenderly. "There's no one on earth who gets me more excited than you. We're not talking about whether or not you have the ability to get me off, but why you're trying to do it in the middle of my mother's fundraiser."

Guilt put her back up. "I guess the thrill is gone. And so early in our marriage, too. I thought that didn't wear off until at least after the first year."

He rolled his eyes. "I literally just told you this is not a conversation about how much I desire you. I'm trying to figure out why you have a seemingly self-destructive need to have sex in public. That's what got us into this marriage in the first place."

So now all this was her fault? "There were two people in that hot tub, Hendrix."

"Willingly," he threw in far too fast and that pissed her off, too. "I'm not pushing blame onto you. I wasn't saying no as you pulled me into that closet at the wedding. But I am right now. Wait."

He tightened his grip on her fingers as he correctly guessed she was about to storm off to…somewhere that she hadn't quite worked out yet.

"Sweetheart, listen to me."

And she was so out of sorts that she did, despite knowing in her marrow she wasn't going to like what he had to say.

"You want me so badly that you can't wait?" he asked. "That's great. I want you like that, too. The problem is that we both use that heat as a distraction. From life, from… I don't know. Crap going on inside. Whatever it is, I don't want to do that anymore."

The earnestness in his expression, his tone, in the very stroke of his fingers over hers bled through her, catching on something so deep inside that it hurt. "I don't do that."

He didn't even have the grace to go along with the lie. "You do. We're cut from the same cloth. Why do you think we were both so willing to go through with this marriage? We understand each other."

Oh, God. That was so true it nearly wrenched her heart from its mooring. If he made her cry, she was never going to forgive him. She'd spent *thirty minutes* on her makeup. "What are you saying?"

His smile did nothing to fix the stuff raging through her chest. "I'm saying let's take our sex life behind closed doors. Permanently. Let's make it about us. About discovering what we can be to each other besides a distraction."

"So there's no more chance of public humiliation, you mean?"

He shook his head, dashing the out she'd handed him. "No. Well, I mean, yes, of course that is a very good side benefit. But I'm talking about removing the reasons why we're both so good at creating scandals. Stop avoiding intimacy and get real with me. At home."

That was the worst idea she'd ever heard in her life. "You first."

He nodded. "I'm at the head of the line, sweetheart. Get in the queue behind me and let's do this ride the way it was intended."

Her lungs hitched. "You're not just talking about laying down a new no-sex-in-public rule. Are you?"

"I don't know what I'm talking about." He laughed self-consciously, finally releasing her fingers to run a hand through his hair. "All I know is that my mom asked me to get married so her campaign wouldn't take a hit and all I could think about was getting you into bed again. Then we made a mutual decision that sex was off the table until after the ceremony. It really made me think about who I want to be when I grow up. An oversexed player who can't control himself? I don't want to be that guy. Not with you."

Stunned, she blinked up at him but his expression didn't waver. He was serious about making changes and somehow, she was wrapped in the middle of all of it. Like maybe he wanted to be a better person because of her. That was… She didn't know what that was, had no experience with this kind of truth.

"So where does that leave us?" she whispered.

He tilted his head until their foreheads touched. "A married couple who's expected at a fundraiser. Can we get through that and then we'll talk?"

She nodded and the motion brought his head up just at the right angle to join their lips. The kiss had nothing to do with sex, nothing to do with heat. It was a sweet encapsulation of the entire conversation. A little tender, a little confused and so much better than she'd have ever dreamed.

Somehow, she floated along behind him as he led her back into the fray and the fact that they hadn't gotten naked meant something significant. Hell if she knew what. Later tonight, maybe she'd get a chance to find out.

Turned out that Roz hadn't actually needed the orgasm to relax after all. Hendrix held her hand like he'd promised and generally stuck by her side through the whole of the fundraiser. The evening wound to a close without one snide comment being wafted in her direction. Whether that was because Hendrix had studiously kept her far away from her father—a fact she couldn't help but notice and appreciate—or because the marriage had really worked to soften society's opinion toward them, she couldn't say.

Ultimately, the only thing that mattered was that she ended the evening on a high she hadn't felt in a long time. Not even sex could compete with the burst of pure gratitude racing through her veins as the limo wheeled them toward Hendrix's house. Their house. It was technically theirs, for now, as he was sharing it with her. No harm in claiming it as such, right?

"I think that was a success, don't you, Mr. Harris?" she commented as he held the door open for her to precede him.

He shut it with a resounding click. "I'm sorry, I missed everything you just said outside of 'Mr. Harris,'" he murmured and propelled her up the stairs with insistent hands on her hips.

She let him because it suited her to get to a place where they could pick up their discussion from earlier. "You like it when I call you Mr. Harris? I can do that a whole bunch more."

"I insist that you do."

Once in the bedroom he sat her down on the bed, knelt at her feet and took enormous care with removing her shoes, unbuckling the straps with painstakingly slow pulls, watching her as he did it. His gaze flickered as he finally slipped off one shoe and then the other. He lifted her arch to his mouth, kissing it sensuously.

It was such an unexpected move that something akin to nerves popped up, brewing inside until she had to say something to break the weird tension.

"We got through the fundraiser," she said. "Is this the part where we're going to talk?"

"Uh-huh," he purred against her foot and dragged his lips up her leg.

It happened to the be the one revealed by the

slit that opened almost all the way to her hipbone, so he had a lot of real estate to cover. Her flesh heated under his mouth, sending an arrow of desire through her core.

"First," he said. "I'm going to tell you how absolutely wild you drive me. Are you listening?"

He nibbled at the skin of her thigh and slid a hand up the inside of her dress, exactly as she'd imagined he would—at the table while they were eating dinner. She'd envisioned it being a huge turn-on to have his hands under her dress while they were sitting there with members of high society, especially given how sanctimonious they'd all been about the photograph. And Hendrix had taken that possibility off the table and opened up a whole different world at the same time.

This wasn't a turn-on because she was putting one over on the high and mighty. It was a turn-on because of the man doing the caressing. Exactly as he'd suggested, taking their sex life behind closed doors put a sheen on the encounter that she couldn't recall ever having felt before.

"I hear you," she whispered. "Tell me more."

His fingers slid higher, slowly working their way toward the edge of her panties and then dipping underneath the hem to knuckle across her sex. She gasped as the contact sang through her, automatically widening her legs to give him plenty of access.

"Wild." He gathered her dress in one hand as

he slid up the other leg to bunch the red silk at her thighs. "Do you have any concept of how difficult it was to tell you no at the fundraiser?"

"Seemed pretty easy to me," she mumbled and immediately felt like a selfish shrew. "But I'm sure it wasn't."

"No," he agreed far too graciously instead of calling her on her cattiness like he should have. "I carried around a boner for at least half the time. This dress…" He heaved a lusty sigh as he trailed a finger from the fabric gathered over her shoulder down over her breasts, which tightened deliciously from no more than that light touch. "I'm going to have to do this the right way."

"Because you have such a habit of doing it wrong?" she suggested sarcastically.

"I mean, I can't take it off. Not yet." He speared her with a glance so laden with heat and implications that her core went slick and achy instantly, even before he put his hands under the skirt and hooked her underwear, drawing off the damp scrap to toss it over his shoulder.

Pulling her to the edge of the bed, he spread her thighs and treated her to the deepest, wettest French kiss imaginable. A moan escaped her throat as he lit her up from the inside out, heat exploding along her skin as Hendrix set fire to every inch of her body. He closed his eyes as he pleasured her and she could scarcely look away from the raw need plastered all over his face.

It should be the other way around. He had his mouth on her in the most intimate of kisses, and she felt herself coming apart as she watched his tongue swirl through her folds. His fingers twined through the silk of her dress, the one he'd given her as a sweet, unexpected gift, and that gave everything a significance she scarcely understood.

The release rolled through her, made so much more powerful by the fact that he was letting her see how much she affected him. He was still telling her how wild he was over her, and she was still listening. When she came, she cried out his name, hands to his jaw because she couldn't stand not touching him as her flesh separated from her bones, breaking her into a million unrecoverable pieces.

His eyes blinked open, allowing him to witness it as she slid into oblivion and it was a horrible shame that he wasn't right there with her. She wanted that, wanted to watch him come apart with abandon.

"Make love to me," she murmured and guided his lips to hers for a kiss that tasted like earth and fire. It was elemental in all its glory and she wanted more.

He got out of his clothes fast enough to communicate how much he liked that suggestion but when he reached for her, she pulled him onto the bed in the same position she'd just been in and straddled him, still wearing the dress.

"I might never take it off again," she informed him as she settled against his groin, teasing him with her still-damp core. Hard, thick flesh met hers and she wanted him with a fierceness she could hardly contain.

He groaned as she arched her back, thrusting her covered breasts against his chest. "It feels divine."

And that was enough of a recommendation for her to keep going, exactly like this. She pulled a condom from the gathered place at her waist, which she'd stashed there earlier in hopes of finding a closet at the fundraiser, but this was far better.

His gaze reflected his agreement, going hot with understanding as he spied the package in her fingers. "I see you attended the fundraiser fully prepared to go the distance."

"Yeah. But it's okay. This is exactly the way our evening was supposed to go." How he'd converted her, she still didn't know. But it sure felt like how this ride should be experienced. If it wasn't, she didn't want to know about it.

Condom in place, she slid down until they were joined and he was so deep inside that there was no room for anything else. He captured her gaze and held it for an eternity, even as he slid his arms around her to hold her tight. It was the most intimate position she'd ever been in with another human being and it was so beautiful her heart ached.

And then it got even better as they moved in tandem in a sensuous rolling rhythm unlike anything she'd ever felt. Her head tipped back as she rode the wave of sensation and Hendrix fused his mouth to her throat, suckling at her skin. He murmured things against it, telling her how much he liked the way she felt, how sexy she was. The pretty words infused her blood, heightening the experience.

The release split through her body almost before she'd realized it was imminent. It was quieter, deeper than the first one. More encompassing. She let it expand, grabbing on to the sensation because it was something she wanted to savor. Hendrix's expression went tense with his own release and he drew it out with a long kiss, perfectly in sync with her in a way she knew in her bones would never have happened if they'd banged each other in a closet.

This was something else, taking their relationship to the next level.

He picked her up and set her on her feet so he could finally remove the dress and then gathered her into his arms to lay spoon style under the covers. She didn't resist, couldn't have. She wanted all of this to be as real as it felt, but as she lay there in the dark listening to her husband breathe, her eyes refused to stay closed.

None of this was going to last. She'd forgotten that in the midst of letting Hendrix prove they could have a closed-door relationship. She'd forgotten that their marriage had become intimate long before they'd signed any papers and she'd let herself get swept away in the beauty he'd shown her.

She did use sex as a distraction, as an avoidance tactic. Because she hadn't wanted to be in this position. Ever. But she'd let him change the dynamic between them.

They were still getting a divorce. She *couldn't* forget that part because it was the theme of her life.

She lost everything important to her eventually and Hendrix fell into that category just as much as anything else. This wasn't the start of a new trend. Just the continuation of an old one that was destined to break her heart.

Nine

Helene made a rare appearance at the office, bringing a huge catered lunch with her that the employees all appreciated. Hendrix let her have her fun as the company still had her name on it even though she'd transitioned the CEO job to him long ago. As the last of the potato salad disappeared from the break room and the employees drifted back to their desks, Hendrix crossed his arms and leaned back on the counter to contemplate his mom.

"What gives?" he asked with a chin jerk at the mostly decimated spread. "You get a large donation or something?"

Her lips curved into the smile that never failed

to make him feel like they were a team. At last, it seemed like they were back on solid ground again.

Sure, she smiled at everyone, because she had the sunniest personality of anyone he'd ever known, but she was still his mom no matter what and he valued their bond more than he could explain.

"Paul Carpenter dumped five million in my lap. You didn't have anything to do with that, did you?"

He shrugged, wishing he could say it was an act of generosity and that she shouldn't read anything into it, but odds were good the donation came with strings. Carpenter had another think coming, if so. Having the billionaire as a father-in-law hadn't checked out like he'd expected. It chafed something fierce to have his hopes realized of being aligned with a powerful old money family, only to find out the patriarch was an ass.

"Not even close. I don't like how he treats Roz. If you recall, I might have given him that impression the last time we spoke at the wedding."

"Well, he's not the only one with a giving soul. The fundraiser was a huge success. I came by to thank you for hanging out with us old people."

Hendrix snorted. The day Helene could be described as old had yet to come. She had boundless energy, a magnanimous spirit and could still give women half her age a run for their money. "You're only seventeen years older than me, so you can stop with the old business. And you're welcome."

"You know what this means, right?" Helene eyed him curiously. "Your marriage to Roz worked to smooth over the scandal. My approval ratings are high. Seems like you did it. I don't know how to say thank you for this enormous sacrifice you made for me."

He grinned to cover the slight pulse bobble at what his mother was really saying—he and Roz had reached their goal much faster than originally anticipated. Her speech had all the hallmarks of what you said as something was winding down. And he did not want to think of his marriage that way. "It was really my pleasure."

His mom stuck her fingers in her ears in mock exasperation. "I don't want to know. This time, keep your sex life to yourself."

"I'm trying." And it was working well. So well, he could scarcely believe how easily he'd slid deeper into his relationship with Roz. They fit together seamlessly and it was nearly too good to be true. Far too good to be talking about ending it already. "I really like her."

God, was he fourteen again? He was an adult who could surely find a better way to describe how his insides got a little brighter at the mere thought of his wife. But what was he supposed to say about the woman he woke up to every morning? Or about how he hadn't yet figured out why his marriage *wasn't* making him run screaming for the hills?

"I can tell," his mom said lightly. "I'm headed to see her next. You wanna come with me?"

His eyebrows shot up automatically. "You're going to see Roz?"

Helene and his wife weren't having lunch any longer even though he'd told Roz repeatedly that it was fine if she built a friendship with Helene. He still felt like he'd nipped that relationship in the bud prematurely. It didn't sit well and if they were mending the fences he'd knocked down, he definitely didn't want to get between them again.

"I am," she confirmed. "I can't put off my promise to her any longer and still sleep at night. So I'm doing the clown thing. Full makeup and all."

"The press will eat it up," he promised and she nodded her agreement.

"Yes, I'm counting on it. It should be quite a circus, no pun intended."

He laughed, glad that despite the many other changes that had been forced on them over the years, they could still hang out and crack jokes with each other. He'd never censored one word to his mother and she was the one person he could be completely real with.

Well, not the only one. He could be real with Roz. He'd never censored anything he'd said to her either, a first. Usually he watched what he said to women because who wanted to give false expectations? But his relationship with Roz required absolute honesty from the get-go and it was a facet of their relationship he hadn't fully appreciated until now.

Tomorrow if he woke up and knew with certainty that he was done, he just had to announce it was time to file for divorce and she'd say okay. It was freeing to know he never had to pull punches with the woman he was sleeping with.

Not so freeing to be contemplating the fact that he'd practically been handed permission to bring up that divorce. He wasn't ready to think about that. They hadn't been married that long and surely Helene would want them to see this thing through a little while longer. Just to be absolutely certain that a divorce wouldn't undo all the good they'd done already.

"I have to admit, I'm intrigued by the whole clown idea," he told her. "But I have that presentation on restructuring the supply chain and I need to do a thorough sweep of the warehouse like I've been threatening to do for weeks."

Helene wrinkled her nose. "That sounds boring."

"Because it is. Being the CEO isn't all curly wigs and water-squirting flowers." Neither was being a political candidate, but she knew he was kidding.

"That's the benefit of being the boss," she reminded him and pushed him ahead of her out of the break room where his admin had started cleaning up the leftover boxes. "You can leave the boring stuff for another day and come watch me be a clown. It's for a good cause. And it's an opportunity to be seen with your lovely bride in a stellar photo op where everyone will not only be dressed but overdressed."

Seeing Roz in the middle of the day for no other reason than because he wanted to held enormous appeal that he chose not to examine too closely. And it was coupled with an opportunity to see what she did on a daily basis unobtrusively. He did have a certain curiosity about her charity. Because... *clowns*. It was such a strange thing to be passionate about.

"Sold." He buttoned his suit jacket. "Let me—"

"Not one foot in your office or you'll never emerge." Helene looped an arm through the crook of his elbow and tugged. "Ride with me in my car. We'll drop you off back here to get your car later."

And that was how he found himself at Carolina Presbyterian Hospital with his mother in clown makeup. The children's ward was a lively place, if not a little depressing. Easy to see why clowns might make the whole thing a tiny bit less awful. God willing, he'd never have to personally empathize with what these families were going through. He made a mental note to write Roz a check, which he should have done a long time ago.

He snuck a glance at Roz from the corner of his eye as he lounged in the spot he'd reserved for himself, which was well out of the way, yet afforded him a front-row seat for the show. His wife was gorgeous, focused and quite possibly the tensest he'd ever seen her, including the time they'd braved the florist, their wedding reception and, his least favorite, the encounter with her father in the hall after nearly being caught with their pants down.

Either she didn't like that he'd accompanied his mother or she was worried that something was going to go wrong with this once-in-a-lifetime opportunity to get buzz for her charity.

While Helene entertained the kids with stuffed animals she'd carried into the hospital in a big bag, Hendrix edged toward Roz, who had yet to acknowledge his existence. Not that he was nursing a teeny bit of hurt over that or anything.

"Hey," he murmured, mindful of the two separate news crews that were covering the gubernatorial candidate's foray into the world of therapy clowning, a thing he'd had no idea had a name, but apparently did.

"Hey." Her mouth pinched back into a straight line that he immediately wanted to kiss away.

Definitely tense and dang it if it wasn't on the tip of his tongue to suggest they find a closet somewhere because she was wound tight. But they weren't *that couple* any longer. For a reason. So he'd have to handle his wife's tension verbally. "You have a problem with me being here?"

"What?" She glanced at him and then immediately flicked her gaze back to Helene. "No. I don't care. It's a free country."

Which was the kind of thing you said when you *did* care but hadn't planned on letting anyone else in on the secret.

"Your shoes are too tight?" he guessed but she didn't smile at the joke.

"This is a big deal, Hendrix. I'm allowed to be nervous."

The sarcasm lacing the edge of her words was pure Roz, but he'd spent far too much time in her company to accept her comment as pure truth. She wasn't nervous. Tense, yes. But it wasn't nerves.

And like what had happened at their engagement party, he was nothing if not painfully aware that he could read her so easily because he was paying attention to *her*, not how best to get under that severe suit she'd donned like armor.

"She's doing fine," he told her with a nod toward his mom. "Come get some coffee with me."

Roz shot him another side-eyed glance, as if afraid to take her gaze off Helene for one second. "I can't leave. This is my charity on the line."

"On the line?" he repeated. "Like if Mom does the wrong thing, it's all going to collapse? You know no one is going to stop letting you do clowns just because she fails to make one of the kids smile, right?"

Her shoulders rolled back a couple of times as if she couldn't find a comfortable stance. "Maybe not. But maybe it's all going to collapse for other reasons."

That wasn't the fierce Rosalind Carpenter he knew. "If it does, that's not on you."

"It is," she hissed back under her breath. "Why do you think I needed your mother in the first place? Not because I thought kids would like to meet the woman who may be the governor by January."

"Will be," he corrected automatically because there was no way Helene was going to fail to reach her goal, not if he had anything to say about it. After all, he'd signed a marriage license to ensure that his mom got to move into the Governor's Mansion. The fact that his marriage had become so much more still wasn't something he had a handle on. "Why don't you clue me in on why Helene is really here if it's not to bring joy to some sick kids?"

Roz's eyes snapped shut and her chest heaved a couple of times through some deep breaths. "Actually, coffee would be good."

Despite being certain she'd found yet another avoidance tactic since she couldn't use sex, he nodded once and put a hand to her waist to guide her out of the room. After all, coffee had been his suggestion, but not because he'd intended to give her an out. It was a little uncomfortable to realize that while he might not be censoring his words with her, that didn't mean she was returning the favor.

And he wanted to know what was swirling beneath her skin. He wanted to know *her*. They might be on the downslide, but he couldn't contemplate letting her go, not right now. There was still too much to explore here.

Instead of taking her to the cafeteria where the coffee would be weak and tepid, he texted his driver to hit the Starbucks on the corner, then found the most private corner in the surprisingly busy children's ward. He let Roz choose her seat and then took the opposite one.

She stared out the window, and he stared at her. The severe hairstyle she'd chosen pulled at her lush features, but nothing could change the radiance that gave her such a traffic-stopping face. When he'd left her this morning, she'd still been in bed, her long dark hair tumbling over her shoulders the way he liked it.

But he didn't think she'd appreciate it if he pulled the pins free right here in the middle of the hospital. "Coffee's on its way."

She nodded. "Thanks. I need it."

"This is the conversation you want to have?"

Her mouth tightened. "I didn't want to have a conversation at all."

"But you needed the air," he guessed and her wince said he'd called it in one. "Roz, I'm not going to bite. If you want to talk to me, I'm not going anywhere. But if you don't, then let's sit here while you collect yourself. Then we'll go back and do clowns with no one the wiser that you had an anxiety attack or whatever."

Her double take was so sharp, it should have knocked her off the chair. "Anxiety attack? Is that what it looked like? Could you tell I was mid-freakout? Oh, God. Did any of the cameras pick it up? They did. Of course they did. They're all over the place and—"

"Sweetheart, you need to breathe now." He gathered up both her hands in his and held them in his lap, rubbing at her wrists as he racked his brain for information about what he'd accidentally triggered with his random comment. "Breathe. Again. Roz. Look at me."

She did and no, he hadn't imagined the wild flare of her irises a moment ago. Something had her spooked. But she was breathing as instructed, though the death grip she had on his hands would leave a mark, particularly where her wedding rings bit into his index finger. Didn't matter. He didn't have any intention of letting her go.

His driver appeared with two lattes, set them on the table and vanished quickly. Hendrix ignored the white-and-green cups in favor of his alternately white-and-green wife, who, if he didn't miss his guess, might actually be about to lose her lunch.

"Um…" How did you go about delicately asking your wife if she had a positive test result to discuss? "Are you feeling faint? Do I need to call a doctor?"

What if she *was* pregnant? A thousand different things flashed through his head in an instant. But only some of them were of the panicked variety. Some weren't that unpleasant. Some were maybe even a little bit awed and hopeful.

"Oh, God, no!" she burst out. "Please don't bother anyone. I'm fine."

"Of course you are," he murmured and rubbed at her wrists again. "But maybe you could give me a little more to go on as to why we're sitting here in the corner not drinking the hot coffee that I got for us?"

She slipped a hand from his before he was ready to lose the contact and palmed her cup, sipped at the contents and shot him a fake smile. "See? Drinking."

"See?" He waved a hand in front of his face. "Still sitting here in the dark about what's going on with you. Roz, we're married. I've touched you in the most intimate places. I've done more illicit, dirty, sinful things with you than with anyone else in my life. You fell asleep in my arms last night. What is all of that but a demonstration of trust? There is nothing you can say to me that would change—"

"I'm afraid of clowns."

* * *

Oh, God. Now it was out there and Roz had no-where to hide. She'd blurted out her deepest secret and even worse, she'd done it in the middle of He-lene's shot in the arm for Clown-Around.

Hendrix wasn't laughing. He should be. There was nothing scary about clowns. Especially not when it was her mother-in-law underneath the makeup. Geez, she'd half thought seeing Helene all dressed up would be the magic bullet to fix all of the crazy going on inside that had only gotten worse the more Roz forced herself to be around the source of her fear.

"Okay." Hendrix's beautiful eyes flashed as he removed the coffee from her grip and recaptured her hand. As if he knew that holding her in place was something she desperately needed but didn't know how to ask for. "That's not what I thought you were going to say."

"No, probably not." Her mouth twisted into a wry smile designed to disguise the fact that she wished she could cry. "I wasn't expecting me to say it, ei-ther. It's dumb, I know."

He shook his head fiercely. "No. What's dumb is that you're holding all of it inside when I'm here. Tell me what I can do, sweetheart."

That's when her heart fluttered so hard that there was no way it could possibly stay behind her rib cage. *Now* she was feeling light-headed and like she might need a doctor to fix whatever he'd just broken inside her.

"Hold my hand," she mumbled because what else was she supposed to say when his impassioned statements might loosen her tear ducts after all?

"I am. I'm not going to stop."

He wouldn't, either. Because he was Hendrix Harris, the hero of her story, who stood up to her father and had such a good relationship with his mother that he'd willingly marry the wild Carpenter daughter with seemingly nothing to personally gain from it. In bed, he worshipped Roz. Out of it, he talked her down. He was everything she'd never have said she wanted—but did—and that was pushing buttons inside that weren't meshing well with clowns.

But at least she didn't feel like she was standing on the edge of a mile-high cliff any longer, legs about to give out as the darkness yawned at her feet. She could breathe. Thanks to Hendrix.

"I started Clown-Around because I needed to stop being afraid." He didn't blink as she blurted out her second-biggest secret, and he didn't interrupt with a bunch of advice on how to fix it. "I really thought it was going to work."

"Facing your fears is a good step," he agreed and shut his mouth expectantly, as if to indicate this was still a conversation and it was her turn again. He was good at that and she didn't mistake it as anything other than a skill.

That or he was just good at being with *her*, and she might appreciate that even more.

It was the thing she clung to as she spilled out the story of her eight-year-old self missing an entire semester of school because no one could figure out how to tell her she wasn't allowed to sit at the bedside of her dying mother.

At first, they'd tried. Her nanny would drive her to school, only to get a call from the headmistress that Roz had snuck out again. Fortunately, her father had found her at the hospital before the police had gotten involved, but his mandate that she not try that trick again had only fueled her need to both defy him and spend time with her mother. Sneaking out of school became great practice for later, when she did it to hang out with boys nearly twice her age.

As she recalled all of it for Hendrix, she didn't leave any of it out, especially not the ugly parts because he deserved to know what was going on with her, as he'd asked to.

"She was so sick," Roz recalled, not bothering to wipe the stream of tears that finally flowed. They'd just be followed by more. "The chemo was almost worse than the cancer and they'd come to get her for the treatments. I wouldn't let her go. There were these clowns."

She shuddered involuntarily, but Hendrix didn't

say anything, just kept rubbing a thumb over the pulse point of her wrist, which was oddly comforting.

"Every day, I imagined that I was helping draw all the poison from her body when I sat by her bedside and held her hand. But they wouldn't let me go with her to the treatments and when she came back, it was like they'd sucked a little more of her life away."

Verbalizing all of this was not helping. If anything, the absolute terror of it became that much fresher as she relived how the two clowns wrenched her hand out of her mother's, with their big fake smiles and balloon animal distractions. They'd been employed by the hospital administration to keep her out of the way as the staff tried to care for her mother. She knew that as a rational adult. But the associations in her head with clowns and the way her mother slipped away more and more each day— that association wasn't fading like the psychologists had said it would.

"And now you know the worst about me," she informed him blithely.

Instead of responding, he dashed away the tears from her cheeks with one thumb, still clinging to her other hand as promised. His strength was amazing, and definitely not a quality she'd have put on her top twenty when it came to men. It was a bonus, particularly since he had twenty out of twenty on the list of what she'd have said would embody her perfect man.

What was she going to do with him?

Divorce him, most likely. Her heart lurched as she forced herself to accept the reality that all of his solid, quiet strength, the strength that was currently holding her together, wasn't permanent. She didn't get to keep things. The clowns were a great big reminder of that, one she needed to heed well.

"So what you're telling me is," he drawled, "that the worst thing about you is that you went through an incredibly traumatic series of events as a child and clowns were in the middle of it. And now they freak you out. Stop me when I get to the part where I'm supposed to cast the first stone."

She rolled her eyes. Miraculously, the fact that he was cracking jokes allowed her to reel back the emotion and take a deep breath. "Yeah, okay. It's not on the same level as adultery. But it's still real and scary and—"

"Something we need to deal with," he cut in, his gaze heavy on her with sympathy and tenderness. "And we will. You know what most people do with fears? They run really fast in the other direction. You started an extremely worthwhile charity while trying to deal with *your* fear. I don't think I've ever been more impressed with a human being in my life than I am with you right now."

Okay, not so much with reeling back the emotions then. The tears started up again as she stared at him. "It's not working, though, in case you missed that part."

He shook his head. "Doesn't matter. We'll try something else. What matters is that you're amazing and you can't erase that by throwing down your failures."

She hadn't done anything special. But he had. She felt hollowed out and refilled all at the same time, and Hendrix was the reason. That scared her more than anything else that had happened today. "I don't think I can go back in there."

Which wasn't the biggest issue but the only one that she could reasonably be expected to address at this point. It was also the most critical.

Nodding, he squeezed her hand. "That makes sense. The problem is that you want to."

How did he see the things inside her so clearly? It was as frustrating as it was extraordinary. It meant that she needed to watch herself around him. If she wasn't careful, he'd pick up on the way her insides were going mushy as he sat with her in the corner of the children's ward holding her hand when he had a multimillion-dollar business to run.

"The problem is that I need to," she corrected. "This is my charity. Your mother is helping me enormously by bringing credibility to my organization."

And it was doubtful she needed to explain that her

credibility was lacking. He understood how scandals affected everything—regardless of whether you deserved it—far better than anyone else in her life.

"Here's an idea," he said casually. "Why don't you be a clown?"

"Say what?" But she'd heard him and the concept filtered through all the angst and fear and found a small snippet of reason, latching onto it with teeth. "You mean with makeup and everything?"

"Sure." He shrugged. "Maybe you haven't been able to fix your fear because you're too far away. You can't just get near your fears. You need to be inside them, ripping the things to shreds, blasting them apart internally."

"Oh, sure, because that's what you do?"

The sarcasm didn't even faze him. He cocked his head and stared straight down into her soul. "Married you, didn't I?"

Before she could get the first of many questions out around the lump in her throat, one of Helene's staffers interrupted them, shattering the intensely intimate moment. Good. They'd gotten way too deep when what she should be doing is creating distance. The last thing she wanted to hear was how freaked he'd been to lose his independence and how great it was that he had an imminent divorce to keep his fears of commitment at bay. It wasn't hard to imagine a player like Hendrix Harris with a little calendar in his head where he ticked off the days until he could shed his marriage.

It was *very* hard, however, to imagine how she'd handle it when that day came. Because losing him was a given and the longer this dragged on, the harder it was going to be to keep pretending she wasn't falling for him—which meant she should do herself a favor and cauterize the wound now.

Ten

Hendrix didn't get a chance to finish his conversation with Roz. Helene's stint as a clown ended faster than anyone would have liked when one of the patients took a scary turn for the worse. Hospital personnel cleared the area and a calm but firm nurse assured Helene that someone would update her on the little boy's status as soon as they knew something.

A somber note to end the day. Hendrix couldn't stop thinking about how short life was, the revelations Roz had made about her childhood and how to pick up their conversation without seeming insensitive. But his own fears that he'd mentioned were as relevant now as they had been before he'd agreed to this marriage.

Even so, he wanted to take a chance. With Roz. And he wanted to talk about how rejection wasn't something he handled well, air his fears the same way she had. But she insisted that he go back to the office with his mom so she could take her car to Clown-Around's tiny storefront and finish some paperwork. He wasn't dense. He'd given her a lot to think about and she wanted to be alone. What kind of potential start to a real marriage would it give them if he pushed her into a discussion before she was ready?

Distracted, he went back to work but he couldn't concentrate, so he drove home early. The expressway was a mess. Bumper-to-bumper traffic greeted him with nothing but red taillights. Of course. Probably because he wasn't supposed to go home.

It didn't matter anyway. By the time he got there, Roz wasn't home yet. He prowled around at loose ends, wondering when the hell his house had turned into such a mausoleum that he couldn't be there by himself. He'd lived here alone for years and years. In fact, it was extremely rare for him to bring a woman home in the first place. Roz had been unique in more ways than one.

By the time Roz finally graced him with her presence, he'd eaten a bowl of cereal standing up in the kitchen, chewed the head off of his housekeeper because she'd dared suggest that he should sit at the empty dining room table, and rearranged the furniture in the living room that he'd used one time in the past year—at his engagement party.

In other words, nothing constructive. He had it bad and he wasn't happy about it.

Her key rattled in the lock and he pounced, swinging the door wide before she could get it open herself. Cleary startled, she stood on the doorstep clutching the key, hand still extended.

"I was waiting for you," he explained. Likely she'd figured that out given his obvious eagerness. "You didn't say you'd be late."

A wariness snapped over her expression that wasn't typically part of her demeanor. "Was I supposed to?"

"No. I mean, we don't have that kind of deal, where you have to check in." Frustrated all at once for no reason, he stepped back to let her into the house. "You weren't late because of me, were you?"

She shook her head. "You mean because of our earlier conversation? No. You gave me advice that I appreciated. I appreciate a lot of things about you."

Well, if that didn't sound like a good segue, he didn't know what would. "I appreciate a lot of things about you, too. On that note, my mother told me earlier today that things are looking really good for her campaign. She thinks the marriage did exactly what it was supposed to."

Roz swept past him to head for the stairs, scarcely

even pausing as she called over her shoulder, "That's great."

A prickle of unease moved down his spine as he followed her, even though he probably shouldn't. She'd come home late and didn't seem to be in a chatty mood. He needed to back off, but he couldn't help himself. This conversation was too important to wait.

"It is. It means that everything we hoped this marriage would do is happening. Has happened. Her donations are pouring in. She helped your charity, and while I guess we don't know the results of that yet—"

"It was amazing," she said flatly and blew through the door of the bedroom to sink onto the bed, where she removed her shoes with a completely blank expression on her face. "I had calls from three different hospitals looking to form long-term partnerships. Helene's already agreed to do a couple more go-rounds for me."

"Wow, that sounds…good?" Her tone had all the inflection of a wet noodle, so he was flying blind.

"Yeah, it's good." She shut her eyes for a beat, pointedly not looking at him. "Things are going well for her. She told me that too when I called her. So we should probably talk about our exit strategy. It may be a little premature, but it's coming faster than I'd assumed and I'd really like to get started on it."

Exit strategy? "You mean the divorce?"

The word tasted nasty in his mouth as he spit it out. It reverberated through his chest, and he didn't like the feeling of emptiness that it caused. A divorce was not what he wanted. Not yet. Not before he'd figured out how to step through the minefield his marriage had become. He couldn't fathom giving up Roz but neither did he want to come right out and say that. For a lot of reasons.

The pact being first and foremost. It weighed so heavy on his mind that it was a wonder his brain wasn't sliding out through his nose.

She glanced up at him for the first time since walking through the door. "I was thinking it might be safe for me to move back to my loft. I miss it. This house is nice but it's not mine, you know?"

He nodded even though he didn't know. Hell, if she'd wanted to live at her loft while they were married, he would have accommodated that. They'd chosen his house for their marital experiment because it had historical significance and there was a possibility they'd do a lot of entertaining.

That possibility still existed. This conversation was extremely premature, in fact. They couldn't get a divorce tonight.

But all at once, he wasn't sure that was his biggest problem. The divorce was merely symbolic of what was happening faster than he could wrap his hands around—the end of his marriage. "You're thinking of moving back to your loft soon?"

She shrugged. "Maybe tomorrow. No one is really paying attention to us anymore now that we're a respectable married couple. It would hardly raise eyebrows if anyone realized I didn't live here anymore."

"It might." The first tendrils of panic started winding through his chest. Roz was already halfway out the door and he hadn't had one second to sort through what he hoped to say in order to get her to stay. "I think it would be a mistake to split up too early. We might still be called on to attend one of my mother's functions. It would look weird if we weren't there as a couple."

"I don't know." Roz rubbed at her forehead again as if this whole conversation was giving her a headache. "I got the impression from your mother everything was fine. Maybe I don't need to be there."

Maybe I need you there.

But he couldn't force his tongue to form the words. What if she said too bad or laughed? If she really cared about him the way he cared about her, she wouldn't have even brought up the divorce. She'd have left that conspicuously out of the conversation. For the first time, she wasn't so easy to read and he was definitely paying attention to *her*, not her panties.

He'd had enough practice at it over the course

of their engagement and marriage that it was second nature now to shove any physical needs to the background while he focused on what was happening between them. He didn't need the ache in his chest to remind him that what was happening had all the hallmarks of the end.

Because he'd taken public sex off the menu of their marriage? Surely not. The ache in his chest intensified as he contemplated her. What a not-so-funny paradox that would be if he'd ruined their relationship by attempting to remove all possibility of scandal. Actually, that was irony at its finest if so. They had a marriage built on sex. Only. Just like he would have sworn up and down was perfect for him. Who wouldn't want that? He was married to a hot woman that he got to sleep with at night. But apparently that wasn't enough for her to stick around.

What would be? The continued irony was that he wasn't even talking to her about that. Couldn't even open his mouth and say *I'm falling for you.*

If he didn't use the word *love* in that sentence, he wasn't breaking the pact, right?

He was skating a fine line between a mutual agreement to end an amicable fixer marriage and laying his heart on the line for her to stomp all over it—and the way this was going, the latter felt like more and more of a possibility.

That couldn't happen if he didn't let on how this conversation had the potential to rip him to shreds.

"We don't have to get divorced right away. What's the hurry? Why not let it ride for a while longer," he said casually as if his entire body wasn't frozen.

She blinked at him. "What would be the point?"

What indeed? All at once, the ache in his chest grew way too strong to bear. Wasn't she the slightest bit sad at the thought of losing what was great about them? The parts that were great were really great. The parts that were bad were…what? There *were* no bad parts. So what was her hurry?

"Because we enjoy each other's company and like the idea of being married?"

She recoiled. "You mean sex."

"Well, sure." Too late, he realized that was probably not the smartest thing to say as her expression closed in. "Not solely that."

But of course she knew as well as he did that sex was what they were both good at. What they'd started their relationship with. What else was there?

The black swirl in his gut answered that statement. There was a lot more here—on his side. But she didn't seem overly interested in hearing about that, nor did she jump up in a big hurry to reciprocate with declarations of her own about what elements of their marriage she might wish could continue.

"I can't, Hendrix," she said simply.

And without any elaboration on her part, his world fell apart.

It was every bit the rejection he'd been so careful to guard against. The only saving grace being that she didn't know how much those three words had sliced through all of his internal organs.

It wasn't Roz's fault that he'd hoped for something legit to come out of this marriage and ended up disillusioned. It was his. And he had to step into the role she'd cast for him whether he liked the idea of being Rosalind Carpenter's ex-husband or not.

It was fine. He still had a decade-long friendship with Jonas and Warren that wasn't in any danger. That was the place he truly belonged and it was enough. His ridiculous need for something real and legitimate with Roz was nothing but a pipe dream.

They didn't talk about it again, and neither did they settle back into the relationship they'd had for that brief period after the wedding. Hendrix hated the distance, he hated that he was such a chicken, hated that Roz didn't seem overly upset about any of it. He moped around until the weekend, when it all got very real.

While Roz packed up her clothes and personal items, Hendrix elected to be somewhere other than the house. He drove around Raleigh aimlessly and somehow ended up at his mother's curb on Cowper Drive, where she lived in a gorgeous house that he'd helped her select. It was Saturday, so odds were good that she was at some event cutting a ribbon or kissing some babies as she rallied the voters. But he texted her just in case and for the first time in what felt like a long while, fate smiled on him. She was home.

He rang the doorbell. Brookes, the head of his mother's security, answered the door. Hendrix nodded at the man whom he'd personally vetted before allowing him anywhere near Helene. Brookes had checked out in every way. On more than one occasion, Hendrix had wondered if there was something a little more than security going on between Brookes and his mom, but she'd denied it.

Given his reaction when Helene and Roz had lunch, he wouldn't have handled sharing his mother in that respect very well, either. He made a mental note to mention to his mother that he'd recently become aware that he was a selfish crybaby when it came to anyone intruding on his territory, and that maybe she should think about dating anyway despite her son's shortcomings.

"Hey, you," his mother called as she came out of her study wearing a crisp summer suit that had no wrinkles, a feat only someone as stylish as Helene could pull off. "I've got thirty minutes before I have to leave for brunch. Unless you want to be my plus one?"

He shrugged. What else did have to do besides watch the best thing that had ever happened to him walk out of his life? "I could do worse."

Her brows drew together as she contemplated him. "What's wrong, sweetie?"

"Why does something have to be wrong?"

She flicked a subtle hand at Brookes, who vanished into the other room. "Not that I don't enjoy seeing you, but when you come by on a Saturday and start talking about a date with your mother like it's a good thing, I'm concerned. Spill it. Did you have a fight with Roz?"

"No fight." There would have to be a difference of opinion for there to be a fight and he'd agreed with every word she'd said. There was no point to continuing this farce of a marriage. "You said yourself that things were fine with your campaign. You even went out of your way to tell us both that. So what else would be the natural conclusion to a fixer marriage but a fast, no-fault divorce once the problem is fixed?"

Besides, he was pretty sure the black swirl in his gut that wouldn't ease meant he'd been right all along to never have a woman in his bed twice. Better all the way around not to fight Roz on her insistence that it was over. What was he supposed to do, open himself up for exactly the same kind of rejection that had devastated Marcus?

His friends wouldn't have an ounce of sympathy for him either, not after he'd violated the pact. Jonas at least might have had some understanding if Hendrix had managed to find someone who loved him back like Jonas had. Warren wouldn't even let him get the first sentence out and would get started on his own brand of rejection. Hendrix would be dealing with Roz's evisceration *and* lose his friends.

Thankfully, he hadn't even tried.

His mother cocked her head. "So, what? You're done with Roz and thought you'd hang out with your mom for the rest of your life?"

"Sure. What's wrong with that?"

He and his mother were a unit. The real kind. Maybe not peanut butter and jelly, but better because they'd been there for each other over the years when neither of them had anyone else. His mom would never reject him.

Nor did she have a life of her own with someone great who took care of her. Guilt swamped him as he wondered if he had something to do with that.

"For a Harris, you're being a moron," she said coolly. "I told you and Roz that my campaign was fine because I wanted to take that out of the equation."

"Well, congrats. You did and now we have no reason to be married. What else would you have expected to be the outcome of that?"

"A marriage, Hendrix. A real one. I didn't come up with the idea of you marrying Roz *solely* to save my campaign. It was a great benefit and I genuinely appreciate it. But I want to see you happy. She's it for you, honey. I could see it in the photograph."

"What you saw was chemistry," he countered flatly before the hopeful part inside could latch onto the idea that he'd missed something crucial in this whole messy scenario. "We have it. In spades. But there's nothing else there."

"That's ridiculous. You might have figured out a way to lie to yourself, but I have thirty years of practice in reading you. I saw you two together. I listened to Roz talk about you. There's more."

On *his* side. Sure. Not hers.

"Doesn't matter," he growled. "She's out. She told me straight to my face that it was over. Unless you're suggesting that I should resort to chaining her up in the basement, I have to accept that it's indeed over. I wasn't given a choice."

Clearly exasperated, Helene fisted her hands on her hips and despite the fact that he'd been taller than her since he'd turned seventeen, she managed to tower over him. "So, let me get this straight. You told her that you were in love with her and that you might have married her to fix the scandal, but now you'd like to see what it looks like if you stay married because you want to. And she said 'forget it, I'm out'?"

He shifted uncomfortably. How had his mother conjured up the perfect speech to describe the things in his heart when he couldn't have spit out those words at gunpoint? "Yeah. Basically. Except not quite like that."

Or at all like that. He hadn't given her the opportunity to hear those things because it was better not to lay it all out. Saying that stuff out loud meant Roz could counter it easily. Who wanted that kind of outright rejection?

"You didn't tell her, did you?" His mother's gentle tone still had plenty of censure in it.

"I don't deal well with rejection," he mumbled.

"Call Channel Five. There's a newsflash for you."

Her sarcasm wasn't lost on him. The fact that he hadn't told Roz meant he *never* had to deal with it. Instead, he was hiding at his mother's house.

He didn't deal well with relationships, either. He'd spent the whole of his life yearning to belong and holding on with a death grip where he did eke out a place. Neither had led to a healthy balance.

"You don't deal well with it because you have no experience with it. Plus it sucks," she told him. "No one wants to stand in line to let another person hand out pain and misery. But sweetie, Roz makes you happy, not miserable. Why don't you want to fight for that?"

"My father…" He swallowed. He hadn't mentioned the bastard in probably fifteen years and he didn't like doing it now, especially as his mother's mouth tightened. "He didn't even know me and he rejected me. How much worse would it be if I told Roz that I wanted to stay married and she said no anyway?"

"Let me ask you this. How bad does it hurt now?"

Horrifically bad. Worse than he'd allowed himself to admit. Talking about it wasn't helping. "Pretty much like a constant stomach ache."

She rubbed at his arm in that comforting way that only moms knew how to do. "That's also what it will feel like if she says no. So you'd be no worse off. But if you tell her and she says yes, how much better will that feel? Also, you should remember that your father didn't reject you. He rejected me. You didn't even exist yet, not as a real live person he could look in the face and then say he didn't want. You can't let someone else's mistakes cause you to make mistakes of your own."

"You think letting Roz go is a mistake?" His gut was screaming *yes* at a million and five decibels, drowning out the very excellent points his mother was making.

"The important question is whether you think that. But I wouldn't have encouraged you to marry her if I didn't think she could be much more than a mechanism to fix a problem. I'm shocked you didn't realize that already." His mother's voice broke unexpectedly and he glanced at her to see tears gathering in the corners of her eyes. "Just when you think your kid can't surprise you... You really were doing this whole thing for me, weren't you?"

He scowled. "Of course. Well, at first. You're the only mom I have and you're the greatest. Why wouldn't I do anything you needed from me?"

It hadn't hurt that marrying Roz on a temporary basis gave him the perfect excuse to avoid rejection. Too bad it hadn't worked out that way.

"Good answer." She grinned through her tears and then turned him toward the door with a little push. "Now I need you to go home and tell Roz to stop packing because you have important stuff to tell her. Do that for me and at some point in the future we'll laugh about how you almost really screwed this up."

His spirit lightened so fast that it made his head spin. She made something hard sound so easy. Hendrix took two steps toward the door and then stopped. "What if—"

"What-ifs are for losers who can't carry the name Harris, sweetie. In other words, not you." She hustled him toward the door in an almost comical one-two shuffle. "I didn't raise a coward and I'm not going to be satisfied until I have grandbabies. So just keep that in mind."

Babies. The same emotions reappeared that had flooded him back at the hospital when he'd had a small suspicion Roz might be sick for reasons that had nothing to do with clowns. That might have been the clincher. He was too far gone to do anything other than take his mother's advice. "More favors? Marriage wasn't enough for you?"

"That's right. And more important, it's not enough for you, either. Chop, chop. I have a brunch to get to."

His mother closed the door behind him and he got all the way to his car before letting loose with the smile he'd been fighting. Helene Harris was one-of-a-kind. And so was his wife. He had to take a chance and tell her how he felt about her, or he'd never forgive himself. This was his best shot at being a part of something that made him happy and he'd given it a pass instead of fighting for it.

Hopefully, Roz was still at home so he could convince her to stay for reasons that had nothing to do with sex and everything to do with a promise of forever.

The moving company Roz had called made short work of transporting the boxes of clothes, shoes and other personal items she'd taken to Hendrix's house. Good thing. She wasn't in any mood to handle logistics right now.

Hendrix had left earlier, probably to go celebrate his forthcoming independence, and the fact that he was gone was good, too. She could leave without an extended goodbye that would likely yank more tears from her depths that she didn't want to lose. The first and second crying jags of the morning had already depleted what small amount of energy she still had after packing the boxes.

What was wrong with her? There had never been a scenario where she wasn't going to lose this marriage. Why was it hitting her so hard? Because she hadn't prepared properly for it to end? Maybe because it had ended so quickly, with almost no protest from the man she'd married, never mind that she'd stupidly begun to hope things might turn out differently.

That was the problem. She'd fallen into this bit of wonderful she'd found with Hendrix and forgotten it would soon vanish like so many other things in her life.

The moving truck pulled away from the front of Hendrix's Oakwood home and there was nothing left for Roz to do except follow it to her loft. Except she couldn't force herself to pull into the parking garage. She kept driving. The moving company had preauthorization with her building security and they were professionals who didn't need a neurotic, weepy woman supervising them.

Clown-Around could always use more attention. The boost Helene had given the organization surpassed Roz's wildest dreams. Becoming a Harris had launched her into a place that being a Carpenter had never touched. In more ways than one. The thought of how often she'd been *touched* as a Harris depressed her thoroughly.

The paperwork on her desk held zero appeal. She scouted around her tiny office for something else to do, finally landing in the supply closet. It could use organizing. All of the clown makeup and props had fallen into disarray after Helene had stopped by, and frankly, the last thing Roz had wanted to do was surround herself with the trappings that still held so many horrible memories.

But she was already so out of sorts that for once, the wigs lining overhead shelves and the multicolored outfits on hangers at her back didn't bother her. They were just costumes. Easily donned and easily taken off. She grabbed one of the wigs and stuck it on her head.

See? Easy. Not scary. Just some fake curly hair in an outrageous color.

All at once, she sank to the ground and put her face in her hands as the sheer weight of everything overwhelmed her.

Clowns hadn't taken her mother from her. Cancer had. For that matter, no one in a red nose had forced her father to stop caring about her—unless she was doing something he disapproved of, which he cared about plenty. Floppy shoes had done nothing to get her in trouble or bring down society's censure over a racy photograph. She'd done all of that on her own.

Clowns weren't the problem. She was. She'd assigned so much blame to the crappy hand fate had dealt her as a child that she'd practically let it ruin her life. It was only because luck had handed her Hendrix Harris on a silver platter that anything good had happened.

She didn't want that to be over. She didn't want to live each day scared to death to assign importance to the man she'd married. Most of all, she wanted to know what it felt like to know she could wake up each day next to someone who got her. Someone who loved her.

She'd been so busy looking for the hammer about to drop on her happiness that she hadn't considered the possibility that there was no hammer. Hendrix had even said they could put off the divorce, yet she'd let herself become convinced it was better to get it over with rather than see what might happen if she stopped assuming the worst. Maybe they could have tried being married for a few more weeks and let things develop. Go a little deeper.

If only Hendrix was here, she'd tell him that's what she wanted before she lost her nerve.

A chime sounded at the front door as someone pushed it open. Great. She'd forgotten to lock it again. She had to get better at remembering that or else move her offices to a more secure location. Anyone could wander in off the street.

But when she popped out of the closet, cell phone in hand in case she needed to dial 911, the nerves in her fingers went completely numb. The phone slipped from her grip and clattered to the parquet flooring.

As if she'd conjured him, Hendrix stood just inside the door, as gorgeous in a pair of jeans and a T-shirt as he was out of them. Because he had the same smile on his face regardless, the one that he was aiming at her now. The same one that had flushed through her on that dance floor at the Calypso Room a million years ago when she'd first caught sight of him.

"Hendrix Harris," she'd murmured then. And now apparently, as she realized she'd spoken out loud.

"Rosalind Harris," he returned easily, which was not even close to what he'd said to her that night in Vegas but almost made her swoon in a similar fashion. "I like what you've done with your hair."

Her fingers flew to her head and met the clown wig. Oh, God. She started to pull it off and then defiantly dropped her hand. "I'm practicing."

"To be a clown?"

She shook her head. "Facing down my shortcomings. How did you know I was here?"

Which was only the first of a whole slew of other questions, ones that she couldn't seem to get out around the lump in her throat. Hendrix was so close that she could reach out and touch him. She almost did. But she'd given up that right because she was an idiot, clearly.

"I didn't. I went to your loft first but the moving guys said they hadn't seen you. So it was worth a shot to come here. I saw your car outside."

"You were looking for me? That's funny. I…" *Need to tell you some things.* But she had no idea how to take the first step. When she'd wished he was here so she could say what was in her heart, she hadn't actually thought that would happen. He was so beautiful and smelled so delicious and familiar that her muscles had frozen. "You could have called."

"I wasn't sure what I was going to say. I, um, drove around a lot so I could practice." His smile reappeared. "I guess we're both doing that today."

Oddly, the fact that he seemed nervous and unable to figure out how to navigate either melted her heart. And gave her the slimmest glimmer of insight that maybe she'd been completely wrong about everything. "Were you practicing something like, 'watching my mom at the hospital made me realize I have a lifelong dream to be a clown'? Because that can be arranged."

Instead of laughing or throwing out a joke of his own, he feathered a thumb across her cheek. "More like I messed up and let you pack all your stuff so you could leave me, when that's not what I want."

Her whole body froze. Except for her heart. That was beating a mile a minute as something bright fluttered through it. "It's not?"

He shook his head once, never letting go of her gaze. "You're my peanut butter *and* my jelly. Without you, I've got two useless pieces of bread that taste like sawdust. I want a chance to see what kind of marriage we can have without all the extra baggage. I mean, not to put too much pressure on you all at once." He hesitated, looking so miserable that she feared he would stop saying these beautiful things. "I'm trying to say that I want—"

"I love you," she blurted out. Oh, God. What was wrong with her that she couldn't stop behaving like a dimwit when it came to this man? "Not that *I'm* trying to put pressure on *you*—"

"I love you, too," he broke in and she was pretty sure the dazed look on his face was reflected on her own. "I'm changing my answer."

"Because you're a dimwit, too?" Maybe she should stop talking. "I mean, I'm a dimwit. Not you. I was scared that I was going to lose you—"

"No, you're right," he agreed readily. "I'm a complete and total dimwit. I have a problem with rejection so I try really hard to avoid it."

"I wasn't— I mean, I would never reject…" Except for when she'd told him she couldn't stay. She should have stayed. What if he'd never come looking for her? She would have missed out on the best thing that had ever happened to her. "I messed up, too. A lot. I should have told you I was falling for you and that I didn't want a divorce."

Something tender filtered through his gaze. "Funny, that's exactly what I practiced saying to you in the car as I drove around the whole of Raleigh. You stole my line."

"So that's it then? I don't want a divorce, you don't want a divorce. We love each other and we're staying married?" It sounded too good to be true, like a situation ripe for being ripped from her hands. Her pulse wobbled. This was the part where she had to calm down and face her fears like an adult who could handle her life. "I have a hard time trusting that all good things aren't about to come to an instant end."

She swallowed the rest, wishing he'd run true to form and interrupt her with his own revelations. But that didn't happen. He did hold out his hand and when she clasped it, the way he squeezed back was better than any time he'd ever touched her, bar none. Because it was encouraging, accepting. A show of solidarity. *I'm here and I'm not going anywhere*, he said without saying a word.

That loosened her tongue fast. A multitude of emotions poured out as she explained how clowns and cancer and rebellion and marriage had all tumbled together in her head. How she wasn't afraid any longer. She wrapped it up by pointing to the wig. "I'm inside my fears. Blasting them apart where they live. You gave me that. That, along with about a million other reasons, is why I can tell you I love you."

Sure, she still didn't want to lose him but she had absolute faith that if that ever did happen—regardless of the reason—she'd find a way to be okay.

"My turn." Hendrix reached up and plucked the wig off of her head, then plopped it onto his own. "This is the approved method to work through all this stuff, right?"

She nodded as the tears spilled over. "You look like a dork."

He just grinned and patted his red curly hair. "I look like a man who has finally figured out the key to dealing with the idiotic crap running through his head. I almost gave you up without a fight because I was convinced you were going to say thanks but no thanks if I brought up the things I was feeling. Color me shocked that you beat me to it."

"Not sorry."

"I'm just going to insist that you let me say 'I love you' first from now on."

"That's a much better marriage deal than the first one you offered me. I accept." Roz fished her wedding rings from her pocket and handed them to him solemnly. "As long as we both shall live?"

He better. She wasn't a serial wife. This was forever and she knew beyond a shadow of a doubt that she'd love him until the day she died.

He slid the cool bands onto her third finger and it was a thousand times more meaningful than the actual wedding ceremony. "I do."

Epilogue

Jonas and Warren were already seated in the corner booth when Hendrix arrived—late, because his wife had been very unwilling to let him out of the shower.

"This seems familiar," he joked as he slid into the seat next to Jonas and raised his brows at Warren. "Down to you being buried in your phone."

Warren glanced up from the lit screen and then immediately back down. "I like my job. I won't apologize for it."

"I like my job too but I like conversing with real people, as well," Hendrix shot back mildly, well aware that he was stalling. "Maybe you could try it?"

With a sigh, Warren laid his precious link to Flying Squirrel, his energy drink company, facedown on the table. "I'm dealing with a crap-ton of issues that have no solution, but okay. Let's talk about the Blue Devils why don't we? Or maybe the Hornets? What's the topic du jour, guys?"

Hendrix picked up his beer and set it back down again. There was no easy way to do this, so he just ripped the Band-Aid off. "I'm not divorcing Roz."

A thundercloud drifted over Warren's face as Jonas started laughing.

"I knew it." Warren put his head in his hands with a moan. "You fell in love with her, didn't you?"

"It's not that big of a deal." Hendrix scowled at his friend, knowing full well that it was a big deal to him. "Jonas did it, too."

Warren drained his beer, his mouth tight against the glass as his throat worked. He put the glass down with a *thunk*. "And both of you are really stretching my forgiveness gene."

"It was a shock to me too, if that helps."

"It doesn't."

Jonas put a comforting hand on Warren's arm. "It's okay, you'll find yourself in this same situation and see how hard it is to fight what you're feeling."

"I'll never go against the pact," Warren countered fiercely, his voice rising above the thumping music and happy hour crowd. "There were—are— reasons we made that pact. You guys are completely dishonoring Marcus's memory."

Marcus had been a coward. Hendrix had only recently begun to reframe his thoughts on the matter, but after seeing a coward's face in the mirror for the length of time it had taken for him to figure out that love wasn't the problem, he knew a little better what cowardice looked like. "Maybe we should talk about those reasons."

Instead of agreeing like a rational person might, Warren slid from the booth and dropped his phone into his pocket. "I can't do this now."

Hendrix and Jonas watched him stride from the bar like the hounds of hell were nipping at his heels. Dealing with rejection did suck, no two ways about it. But he was getting better at it because he wasn't a coward, not any longer. He was a Harris through and through, every bit his mother's child. Helene had raised him with her own special blend of Southern grit and he'd turned out okay despite never knowing his father. He was done letting that disappointment drive him to make mistakes.

"Welcome to the club." Solemnly, Jonas clinked his glass to Hendrix's and they drank to their respective marriages that had both turned out to be love matches in spite of their bone-headedness.

"Thanks. I hate to say it, but being a member of that club means I really don't want to sit around in a bar with you when I could be at home with my wife."

Jonas grinned. "As I agree with the sentiment, you can say it twice."

Hendrix made it to his house in Oakwood in record time. Their house. His and Roz's. She'd moved back in and put her loft up for sale even though he'd told her at least four times that he'd move in with her. His Oakwood place was a legitimate house but wherever Roz was made it home.

He found her in the bedroom, spread across the bed. Naked.

"Thought you'd never get here," she murmured throatily. "I was about to send you a selfie to hurry you along."

"So our next scandal can be a phone-hack leak of our personal photo album?" His clothes hit the floor in under thirty seconds.

"No more scandals. We're a respectable married couple, remember?" Roz squealed as he flipped her over on the bed and crawled up the length of her back.

"Only in public. Behind closed doors, all bets are off."

She shuddered under his tongue and arched in pleasure. "See what you've done to me? I'm a total sex addict, thanks to you. Before we got married, I was in the running for most pious fiancée alive."

"Not sorry." As much as he enjoyed Roz's back, he liked her front a lot better. That's where her eyes were and he'd discovered a wealth of intimacy in them when they made love, an act which he planned to repeat a million more times. He rolled her in his arms and sank into her.

She was his favorite part of being married.

* * * * *

Don't miss the first IN NAME ONLY book,
Jonas's story
BEST FRIEND BRIDE

and look for Warren's story,
coming in January 2018
CONTRACT BRIDE

And for more of Kat Cantrell's sexy, emotional
style, pick up these other titles!

THE THINGS SHE SAYS
MARRIAGE WITH BENEFITS
PREGNANT BY MORNING

Available now from Harlequin Desire!

***

If you're on Twitter, tell us what you think of
Harlequin Desire! #harlequindesire

COMING NEXT MONTH FROM

HARLEQUIN®
Desire

Available November 7, 2017

#2551 THE TEXAN TAKES A WIFE
Texas Cattleman's Club: Blackmail • by Charlene Sands
Erin Sinclair's one-night stand with sexy cowboy Daniel Hunt is just what she needs. But when she offers to help out a friend and ends up working with someone *very* familiar, she'll soon learn just how determined a cowboy can be!

#2552 TWINS FOR THE BILLIONAIRE
Billionaires and Babies • by Sarah M. Anderson
Real estate mogul Eric Jenner is more than willing to work with his childhood friend Sofia. The single mom needs to provide for her adorable twins. But will combining business and pleasure lead to love...or to heartbreak?

#2553 LITTLE SECRETS: HOLIDAY BABY BOMBSHELL
by Karen Booth
Hotel heiress Charlotte Locke vows to best her commitmentphobic ex Michael Kelly in a business battle. But when he learns she's having his child, he'll have to convince her he'll do right by their child—and her heart—or risk losing her forever.

#2554 EXPECTING A LONE STAR HEIR
Texas Promises • by Sara Orwig
To fulfill a promise, US Army Ranger Mike Moretti goes home to Texas to work on the Warner ranch. His attraction to the owner—his friend's widow—is a temptation he can't resist, and then she announces a little surprise...

#2555 TWELVE NIGHTS OF TEMPTATION
Whiskey Bay Brides • by Barbara Dunlop
Mechanic Tasha Lowell is not his type. She's supposed to be repairing CEO Matt Emerson's yacht, not getting under his skin. But when a charity-ball makeover reveals the sensuous woman underneath the baggy clothes, Matt knows he must have her...

#2556 WRANGLING THE RICH RANCHER
Sons of Country • by Sheri WhiteFeather
When reclusive rancher Matt Clark, the troubled son of a famous country singer, confronts the spunky Libby Penn about her biography of his estranged father, anger and distrust might be replaced with something a whole lot more dangerous to his heart...

YOU CAN FIND MORE INFORMATION ON UPCOMING HARLEQUIN® TITLES, FREE EXCERPTS AND MORE AT WWW.HARLEQUIN.COM.

HDCNM1017

Get 2 Free Books,
Plus 2 Free Gifts—
just for trying the Reader Service!

HARLEQUIN *Desire*

SPECIAL EXCERPT FROM

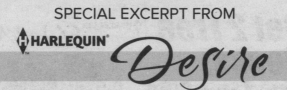
HARLEQUIN™ *Desire*

To fulfill a promise, US Army Ranger Mike Moretti
goes home to Texas to work on the Warner ranch.
His attraction to the owner—his friend's widow—is a
temptation he can't resist, and then she announces a
little surprise...

Read on for a sneak peek of
EXPECTING A LONE STAR HEIR
by USA TODAY bestselling author Sara Orwig,
the first book in her new **TEXAS PROMISES** series.

As Mike stepped out of the car, his gaze ran over the
sprawling gray stone mansion that looked as if it should
be in an exclusive Dallas suburb instead of sitting on a
mesquite-covered prairie.

After running his fingers through his wavy ebony hair,
Mike put on his broad-brimmed black Stetson. As he strode
to the front door, he realized he had felt less reluctance
walking through minefields in Afghanistan. He crossed the
wide porch that held steel-and-glass furniture with colorful
cushions, pots of greenery and fresh flowers. He listened
to the door chimes and in seconds, the ten-foot intricately
carved wooden door swung open.

He faced an actual butler.

"I'm Mike Moretti. I have an appointment with
Mrs. Warner."

"Ah, yes, we're expecting you. Come in. I'm Henry, sir.
If you'll wait here, sir, I'll tell Mrs. Warner you've arrived."

"Thank you," Mike replied, nodding at the butler, who turned and disappeared into a room off the hall.

Henry reappeared. "If you'll come with me, sir, Mrs. Warner is in the study." Mike followed him until Henry stopped at an open door. "Mrs. Warner, this is Mike Moretti."

"Come in, Mr. Moretti," she said, smiling as she walked toward him.

He entered a room filled with floor-to-ceiling shelves of leather-bound books. After the first glance, he forgot his surroundings and focused solely on the woman approaching him.

Mike had seen his best friend Thane's pictures of his wife—one in his billfold, one he carried in his duffel bag. Mike knew from those pictures that she was pretty. But those pictures hadn't done her justice because in real life, Vivian Warner was a downright beauty. She had big blue eyes, shoulder-length blond hair, flawless peaches-and-cream complexion and full rosy lips. The bulky, conservative tan sweater and slacks she wore couldn't fully hide her womanly curves and long legs.

What had he gotten himself into? For a moment he was tempted to go back on his promise. But as always, he would remember those last hours with Thane, recall too easily Thane dying in a foreign land after fighting for his country, and Mike knew he had to keep his promise.

His only hope was that he wouldn't be spending too much time with Thane's widow.

Don't miss
EXPECTING A LONE STAR HEIR
by USA TODAY *bestselling author Sara Orwig,*
available November 2017 wherever
Harlequin® Desire books and ebooks are sold.

www.Harlequin.com